Changing the Rules

Sindee Lynn

Passionate Writer Publishing

Indiana

Passionate Writer Publishing

www.passionatewriterpublishing.com

All characters in this book are fictitious, and any resemblance to real persons, living or dead, is purely coincidental.

©2009 Sindee Lynn

ISBN 13 978-0-9843504-5-2

ISBN 10 0-9843504-5-4

All rights reserved. Published in the United States of America. No part of this publication may be reproduced, stored in a retrieval system or transmitted in any form or by any means, electronic, mechanical, photocopying, recording or otherwise without the written permission of the author or publisher.

Manufactured in the United States of America.

First Edition

Dedication

This book is dedicated to my friend, Jen, for planting the idea for this story in my head and to my friend, Vickie, who convinced me to try just one more publisher. Thank you.

Changing the Rules

Chapter 1

"Hold the elevator please."

Sasha Jordan called out as she came through the revolving doors of Presco Financial. Her heels clicked across the marble covered entryway as she rushed towards the elevators.

"Please hold the doors," she called again but it was barely a whisper.

Her heart was pounding in her ears from her walk, which had been more of a run, across the largest parking lot she'd ever seen. Her interview was in less than twenty minutes and she could not be late. The doors whooshed closed just as she got to them.

"Dammit," she cursed under her breath.

She fought the urge to stomp her foot in frustration. It would only cause more pain to her already aching feet. All she longed for was to find somewhere to sit down and catch her breath but she couldn't afford the luxury. A scream of frustration built at the back of her throat. Things had been going wrong since she'd woke to the ringing of the phone. Mistaking it for her alarm clock she'd reached out and swatted at it absently. When it didn't stop she'd shot straight up in bed. It had been non stop since her feet had hit the floor. It was definitely not how she'd planned the day going when rehearsing it in her head. In all of the checking and double checking last night, not once had it dawned on her to make sure her alarm was set. If it hadn't been for her sister, B.J., calling to wish her good luck she'd probably still be sleeping.

Ding… She looked up to see the elevators doors whoosh open once again.

"Oh thank God."

Sending up a silent prayer of thanks, Sasha stepped inside and pushed the button for her floor before retreating to one corner of the elevator. She took a few precious moments to regain some control over her errant thoughts and to get back into the zone. A few more mumbled confidence builders and she was headed back to the happy place where she was supposed to be. Sure things hadn't gone as planned but that was in the past. She was well on her way to obtaining the job of her dreams and no other reality mattered. A smile broke free as a sense of calm came upon her for the first time since she'd bounded out of bed.

Changing the Rules

In control once more, she began looking for the business card with her interviewer's name on it within the confines of her soft leather briefcase. After a few minutes of fruitless searching, she blew out a puff of air and with it went her happy place. Was anything going to go as it should today? She closed her eyes and took a deep breath. Okay girl you have got to pull it together. Just because things started out rocky and don't appear to be getting any better and everything that can go wrong is going wrong and … Sasha paused in her mental ramblings and lifted her head slowly. What was that smell? Breathing deeply once more, she barely had time to catch herself before a sigh of extreme pleasure passed her lips. It had to be coming from somewhere in the elevator. Glancing around she found the source quickly in the only other occupant in the elevator with her. Wow. How could she have missed him? He looked to be over six feet tall with wavy dark brown hair. His attention was facing forward which offered her an excellent view of his perfect profile. His hair came over his forehead, just barely touching his eyebrows, straight nose and perfectly sensuous lips. A strong jaw line led into the most perfectly shaped man's chin. She wondered if it had a cleft. She'd always been a sucker for a cleft since she'd seen her first Michael Douglas movie. The casual way he leaned against the elevator wall spoke volumes. Not a care in the world. Here was a man who appeared to be very much in control of what was going on around him. Her gaze moved down to the strong set of his shoulders and the way his suit jacket fit perfectly over them, had to be tailored and expensive. It reeked of money. As if feeling her gaze upon him, the man in question turned his head to glance in her direction, a small smile on his face. Sasha's face flamed with embarrassment and she turned away quickly.

God girl get out much, she scolded herself. *You act as if you've never seen a man before.* Her spine stiffened at the internal insult. She made an effort to pull her mind back to the task at hand. The job which had brought her here this morning. And it wasn't just any old job. It was what she'd been working for all these years and with one of Chicago's most well known banking institutions. That's what she needed to remember and stop drooling over some random stranger in an elevator who she would more than likely never see again. So no matter how good looking he is. She snuck a peek at him from under her lashes. Or how absolutely gorgeous he looked leaning against that wall. She needed to focus on the task at hand. But damn what she wouldn't give to know if he looked as good out of clothes as he did in them. And those hands, which were clenching and unclenching at his side. Clench. Release. Clench.

Changing the Rules

Release. Her cunt muscles began to move in rhythm with his fingers. Her stomach tightened with each clench as her body reacted. Her breathing became ragged as she tried to regain control but thoughts of how much she wanted to feel the roughness of those hands graze against her sensitive skin took over. Her breathing faltered over an image of herself lying on her soft Egyptian sheets writhing in pleasure as the hands of this man moved slowly up the inside of her parted thighs. She could almost feel those fingers caressing areas long neglected. Her gaze traveled back up to his side profile. Something safer than those dangerous hands hanging at his sides. She blinked. Though his head remained face forward she could feel his eyes upon her. Oh there was definite interest. Not knowing where the strange emotions taking control were coming from, Sasha raised her head and stared openly at the man across from her. There was no way she could hide the heat in her gaze. She typically wasn't this bold but it was as if she couldn't help herself. Slowly he turned in her direction. The slanted grin on his face told her he'd known she was watching him. And he knew the reason. He was even better looking than she'd initially thought from his profile. The heat in the gaze staring back at her had her pulse and heart rate competing to see which could beat the fastest. She was barely able to stand there and allow his appreciative gaze to roam over her from head to toe. Sasha couldn't help but wonder what he saw. As much as she wanted him to see a voluptuous and sexy African–American woman in front of him, she had to be honest. With her petite stature, standing a little under five feet five inches with barely a handful of breasts, she was certain voluptuous was not the first words that came to mind when looking at her.

Her stranger took a step in her direction and she stopped breathing. His hand reached out towards her. All she could do was stand there. Everything was moving in slow motion as she waited holding her breath in anticipation of his touch.

"Umm excuse me. I believe this is your floor."

Sasha's eyes snapped open. She looked around trying to get her bearings. Her shocked gaze immediately flew to the man still leaning against the elevator wall across from her. Embarrassment clogged her throat as she stumbled from the elevator without a backwards glance or a word of thanks. She walked unsteadily down the hall. What the hell had just happened? One minute she'd been looking at him and the next…? What? Had it all been her imagination? His look of interest? His reaching out to her? Her head was reeling from all the odd emotions moving through her. What had come over her? She had forgotten everything else around her. She paused and took a deep calming breath. It took a moment for her to quiet her rampant thoughts, but finally blessed silence reigned. There was no need to dwell on what was now in the past. It was over. It was just a momentary… a momentary… Oh God what did she call it. She wracked her brain but still came up empty. So she grabbed for what she knew for certain…. The reason she was here. She just needed to remember what had brought her here this morning. Yeah just remember why you are here, she told herself firmly. The job. But no sooner had her brain reached for that one small piece of sanity, than a vivid image of the man from the elevator invaded her thoughts. There had been something about him drawing her to him. Something calling to her deep down in the pits of her being. The thought was dismissed with a shake of her head. The idea was completely absurd. He was nowhere close to being her type. Sasha Jordan did not do white men. It was her number one rule.

Placing her briefcase carefully on the large vanity, she gripped the sides of the sink and practiced several deep breathing exercises. She knew she was wasting precious minutes she didn't have but she felt if she didn't regain control now all would surely be lost for her interview. When she felt more herself, she raised her head to stare at her reflection in the mirror. She wasn't prepared for what she saw. Her lipstick was all but gone and a sheen of perspiration dotted her forehead. She looked flustered. Placing her hands to her cheeks, they were hot to the touch. It had to be due to her earlier sprint across the parking lot. What other reason could it possibly be? She carefully avoided making eye contact with her reflection, sure the lie would be written clearly in the brown gaze staring back at her. When she was sure she could meet her own gaze once more, she turned her attention to repairing the damage done to her appearance. She brought her hand to her hair, which was pulled back in a severe twist against the nap of her neck secured by a large clip. She absently smoothed invisible strands back in place. There was a slight trembling in her fingers. It had to be just a few nerves over her pending interview. Glancing at her watch instead of into the mirror where the truth would be reflected, she realized she was quickly running out of time before her interview. Her rule of being there at least fifteen minutes early had already been blown. The best she could hope for now was to be on time. She quickly touched up her make-up and took a step back to study what she saw. She tried to imagine what her interviewer would see upon first sight.

    For her interview she had chosen a navy blue pants suit with a matching jacket that had been nipped and tucked to fit her petite figure perfectly. Blue was one of her favorite colors and complimented her caramel coloring. She'd paired it with a cream colored silk blouse. The outfit was one of many others in her closet. These were what she considered her power suits. A pair of medium heels rounded out her outfit. It was just a good thing she'd had the forethought to gather her things last night.

Putting her make-up away she caught her reflection again. People had always told her she looked much younger than her thirty-five years with her hair down therefore she typically wore it as it was now. Being petite in stature, at barely five feet four inches in height, was disadvantage enough. She didn't need anything else, like a youthful appearance, to undermine a client's confidence in her ability to do her job. But nothing about this day had gone as planned so she wasn't really surprised when she removed her clip and ran her fingers through the many tiny braids adorning her head. The curls from the previous weekend were still there and she had to admit it definitely looked prettier down. But she was going for full on confident today especially given all the slip ups which had occurred this morning so far. She pulled her hair back preparing to secure it once again at the base of her neck, when she suddenly released it. As she ditched her clip at the bottom of her briefcase and arranged her hair she told herself it had nothing to do with the possibility of meeting her elevator man in the halls of Presco. Her hand stilled. How had her thoughts suddenly gone to him? She didn't have time for this and refused to think of him any longer. After giving herself the final once over she closed her eyes and attempted to center her mind on the task at hand. Things may not have started off as planned but all was not lost. Her dream job was within her reach and she would not be walking out of this building without it. Sasha's eyes snapped open. She was glad to see the confident gaze of the African-American woman who normally resided within her body finally make an appearance.

She turned her attention to the task of locating the business card with the information regarding her interviewer on it. It would definitely not make a good first impression if she didn't know the person's name. Ah, there it was. Michael Shaunessy, Director of Finance, Presco Financial.

"Well, Mr. Shaunessy, I hope you are ready because I am definitely ready for this job," she told her reflection before turning to leave.

Her stride was confident as she walked down the hall towards her destination. A soft smile lingered at her lips. Calm had finally come back to her and man was she glad. No longer were thoughts of a tall well muscled man invading her mind. Her step faltered slightly as her brain brought an image of the man in question to the forefront. She wondered if he worked in the building. Yeah, he works in the mailroom. Now get your head back to the business at hand, she told herself firmly as she approached the receptionist's desk outside of the director's office.

"Good morning. May I help you?" asked the young woman sitting behind the desk.

Eyeing the receptionist skeptically, Sasha managed to return her smile. The young lady at the desk was wearing a form-fitting pink blouse with a V-neck that plunged well below what could be considered business attire. The globes of her voluptuous breasts pushed against the confines of the blouse. It took everything within her not to glance down at her own less than impressive chest. It didn't take a rocket scientist to figure out why she had more than likely been hired. She probably couldn't even type, Sasha thought a little cattily. The genuine smile on the woman's face made her feel immediate shame for her thoughts. Maybe she was a relative. There was nothing wrong with a little nepotism.

"Yes, I have a ten o'clock appointment with Mr. Shaunessy. My name is Sasha Jordan."

"Yes Ms. Jordan there has been an unexpected change in your interview. I tried to reach you this morning before you left home but I wasn't able to."

She briefly recalled the phone ringing as she'd been speed racing through her morning routine. She'd figured it was merely one of her other friends calling to offer support and had ignored it. Now she wished she'd taken the time to at least look at the caller id. Maybe she'd been calling to reschedule and this whole horrible morning might never have happened. And miss the chance to meet Mr. Elevator Man? Her mind questioned. No way. She ignored it and focused on what else was being said.

"Mr. Shaunessy is unexpectedly out of the office today. So your interview will be held on the forty-second floor. Once you exit the elevators, go to the end of the hall and check in with the secretary there and she will assist you."

Hmph. Okay so she would have her interview after all.

"Thank you," She replied absently.

As she walked away, the soft rhythm of clicking keys sounded from behind her. She glanced over her shoulder to see the receptionist's fingers flying over the keyboard. A smile broke free as she walked back down the hallway to the elevators. Her friend, Caitlyn, was always telling her to stop being such a snob and so quick to judge people. Especially when it came to women with bigger breasts than hers.

Changing the Rules

Entering the elevator, she glanced around and wondered if this was the same one from earlier. Against her will she inhaled deeply. Her breath left her in a deep sigh. Was he still in the building? Had he been on his way to meet someone? An image of a woman equally as beautiful as the man she was thinking of came to mind. An immediate frown puckered her brow. Maybe he was meeting his wife. Or his mistress. Sasha shook her head to clear the thoughts. There was no time to be wasting with errant thoughts of a man she would never see again. If she wanted to think about a man, she should be thinking about her neighbor, Louis Wainwright.

For months she'd been waiting for him to spare her more than a friendly wave from the other side of the street. Their hurried conversation from this morning came back to her. Dammit she wished she'd had time to lay some more ground work but there had just been no time. Of all the mornings for him to decide to come across the street. Irritation flashed across her face before she let it go. In his defense he hadn't known she'd been running late and obviously her hints hadn't worked either. Nor apparently put him off if the look of interest when he'd waved bye was anything to go on. Now there was husband potential and if she played her cards right. Sasha hunched her shoulders. Who knew what could happen. But leaning against the wall of the elevator, the image pushing its way to the forefront was not that of Louis but of "him". She couldn't help but recall how his eyes had sparkled with an unreadable expression when he had informed her they were on her floor. Had she imagined it or had she heard him release a sigh as she'd been leaving? She closed her eyes and could almost smell his cologne.

When the elevator doors slid open, Sasha straightened and pulled her wayward thoughts back to the present. The short walk to the desk at the end of the hall was not enough time to completely rein them in but nonetheless, she walked up to the desk with purpose. The woman sitting there reminded her of a bulldog protecting its domain. Her brown hair was streaked with gray and pulled back in a severe bun at the base of her neck much like the one she'd just pulled down. Thank goodness for divine intervention she thought. Wire frame glasses were perched on the tip of the woman's nose as she surveyed Sasha over the top of them. There was no warm greeting as there had been from the woman downstairs. But unfazed she put on her biggest and brightest smile.

"Good morning. I had a ten o'clock appointment with Mr. Shaunessy but his office directed me here. My name is Sasha Jordan."

There was no return smile.

Changing the Rules

"You will be meeting with Mr. Matthews, the CFO of the company. Mr. Matthews, however, has just arrived at the office. So if you would please have a seat, he will be with you shortly."

Knowing when she had been dismissed, Sasha turned on her heels and headed for the closest chair. The CFO of the company. Okay it was no big deal, she told herself. After they couldn't reach her this morning they'd needed someone to step in. More than likely he had a set of standard questions to ask and then he'd pass the information off to Mr. Shaunessy. She was in the midst of her latest pep talk when the doors of the office opened behind her. Dammit. She shouldn't have sat with her back to the door. She liked to make eye contact on first meeting. Oh well, she thought, standing. Smile in place. Deep breath. Sasha paused. It couldn't be. She inhaled again. Her eyes drifted closed as memory took over. It was the same smell from earlier in the elevator. It must be a popular cologne or something. One she wasn't familiar with. Holding her breath, Sasha slowly turned. Her jaw grew slack in shock as her brown gaze roved over the man who had all but consumed her thoughts since she'd first laid eyes on him this morning. It didn't take long to realize she had not imagined his earlier affect on her. She could easily say she was looking at the best looking white man she had ever seen. And he was the CFO of Presco Financial and her interviewer. Her stomached dropped.

"Ms. Jordan?"

Sasha nearly jumped out of her skin when he called her name. God did it have to sound so good. Unsteady legs moved in his direction. The whole time she tried to reassure herself she could do this but the moment recognition dawned in his blue gaze she wasn't so sure anymore. She swallowed uneasily. The wider his smile got the more her apprehension grew. She now regretted her impulsive decision to leave her hair down. She felt vulnerable with it framing her face. But then that vulnerable feeling could just as easily be caused by the way the man standing in front of her was looking at her. This was crazy she screamed inside before giving herself a mental shake. The least she could do was accomplish basic manners. With great effort she forced the smile back to her face and thrust her hand forward.

"Good morning, Mr. Ma - ...,"

Her voice trailed off. Sensations shot threw her fingers and up her arm where they came into contact with his. The feeling spread across her chest. She fought the urge to jerk her hand from his grip, though she doubted she'd have been successful. His firm hold kept her fingers hostage within his.

Changing the Rules

Nervously clearing her throat, Sasha tried again. She raised her gaze to meet his.

"Good morning Mr. Matthews."

Chapter 2

Dylan Matthews looked down at the petite woman standing in front of him and couldn't believe his luck. It was the woman from the elevator. He didn't know if he should thank his lucky stars or curse them. This pint size woman had been the cause of a very painful hard on which was even now threatening to come back to life. By the time he'd reached his office his body and his temper had both been flaring to new heights. He had found himself desperately wishing he could go back home for a series of cold showers. Or find the woman from the elevator and fuck her until his body was spent. A slow smile came to his face as he continued to gaze down at the woman he now had a name for. Sasha Jordan.

"Good morning, Ms. Jordan. I'm Dylan Matthews and it's my pleasure to meet you," he finally replied realizing he'd just been standing there staring at her.

Glancing down at the hand still held captive in his he realized he didn't want to release it. But he had to. The feeling of loss caught him off guard as he caught her gaze once more.

"If you will take a seat in my office I will be with you momentarily."

He stepped aside so she could pass into his office.

His gaze followed the gentle sway of her hips as she walked into his office. A small smile came to his face. Perhaps this wouldn't be such a bad day after all.

When he woke this morning and realized it was later than anticipated, his first call had been to Carla, his secretary, to let her know. That's when he'd been informed Michael had been called away. There had been no need for Carla to tell him Michael's absence meant he'd have to take over the interview scheduled for this morning. They had discussed Sasha Jordan in great detail over the weekend. She was the closet they'd come to finding a qualified candidate for a position they'd been trying to fill for seven long months. So Dylan had rushed through his morning routine and then fought rush hour traffic. When he had finally arrived at the office he'd been met with the closed sign on the private garage under the building reserved for executives of the company. He'd been irritable and regretting having gotten out of bed as he'd leaned against the wall of the elevator attempting to catch his breath from his two mile hike across that god awful parking lot. As the doors were closing and he was considering suggesting a shuttle service for their employees at the next board meeting, he had looked up and seen Sasha rushing across the lobby towards the elevator. She'd looked out of sorts and almost frantic. He'd heard her curse just as the doors had closed and it had brought a smile to his face. To think someone else was having as bad of a day as he was had somehow cheered him a little.

He turned to his secretary.

"Carla, call Morgan and tell him we'll have to reschedule this morning's meeting."

Glancing towards his open door, he could see the rigid set of her shoulders as she sat in the chair across from his desk. He wondered what she was thinking. Did she remember him from the elevator ride? He sure as hell hoped so because he remembered her. Every softly sighing, heated gaze of her.

"And hold my calls," he said turning and walking away before Carla could voice the protest he saw rising on her lips.

Dylan moved into the office and closed the door behind him. Sitting down, he glanced down at the file he had found on his desk upon his arrival. When he'd first glanced at the name, Sasha Jordan, he'd tried to picture what the person would look like. He'd pictured someone tall with strong features and he had to admit he'd conjured up someone white or perhaps of European heritage. He took in the woman sitting across from him and could have laughed at how off the mark he had been. The real Sasha Jordan couldn't have been any taller than five foot five and he may have been giving her an inch or two. He'd felt like a giant while standing beside her petite frame a few moments ago. Her touch had been soft as they'd shook hands. His body hardened painfully as his mind wondered what other parts of her body might be soft to the touch.

Earlier, in the elevator, it had taken every bit of willpower he possessed not to push her against the wall and kiss those luscious sighing lips. He had watched mesmerized as she'd gnawed on them, effectively eating away at her lip stick and gotten harder by the minute. Did she have any idea what those looks had done to him? And God those soft sounds he was sure she hadn't known he'd heard. His body was still humming with desire. From the tension he could feel radiating off her right now, he knew she had to feel it. Hell it was on the tip of his tongue to ask her and get it out of the way. How the hell was he ever going to get through this interview? He had never been this attracted to any woman. The fact she was black made no difference to him. In his philosophy, a woman was a woman. He had never dated a black woman before, but he was making definite plans to change that very soon. There was something about this woman that called to him and he planned to answer.

***

Sasha sat in her chair with her legs crossed. She fought for composure she was far from feeling. Why was he staring at her like that? Didn't he have any questions to ask her? She was here for an interview after all. He'd been pretending to focus on the folder in front of him for what seemed like forever. She may not have seen him raise his gaze her way but she sure as hell felt each time his eyes fell upon her. She was sure he had recognized her earlier from the elevator. And no matter how many times she told herself it didn't matter just the thought he had been aware of what she had been thinking during their brief ride up was enough to cause her to want to die right on the spot. Dammit she hated being in situations like this where she didn't know what to do or how she should proceed. She fought the urge to fidget in her seat as the silence continued. She glanced around his office in hopes of taking her mind off of the man in front of her. Had it been any other man sitting across from her, Sasha was positive she would have been able to relax and enjoy the silence, but it wasn't any other man and relaxing was the last thing she found herself able to do.

Changing the Rules

Her gaze lit upon several framed pictures adorning the walls. Some of the people in them she recognized from photos she'd seen in the newspaper. Her nose almost wrinkled in disapproval before she caught it. To have your life played out on the front pages of the society section was definitely not the life for her. She paused. Her gaze darted to his before returning to the photos once more. Of course. Why hadn't she recognized him from earlier? Even after knowing his name it hadn't clicked for her. Dylan Matthews, CFO of Presco Financial had been the "it" boy up until a few months ago. Everywhere he went had been documented over the last several years. The society pages of The Tribune had become just as bad as those Hollywood tabloids in recent years complete with gossip columns and speculations running rampant over what Chicago's rich and famous were doing. And Mr. Matthews had been one of their favorites. His being the youngest CFO to be named to a bank the size of Presco had even made national news when he'd been appointed the position four years ago. How many times had he won bachelor of the year? Sasha just managed to tamp down on her laughter. Her gaze moved to the other pictures of people who with their striking resemblance to the man still sitting quietly in front of her could only be family. She couldn't help but notice the pride used in displaying several awards he had received. They were ensconced in a glass case sitting upon a marble base in the corner of the room to her left. Shifting slightly in her chair, her gaze came to finally rest on the black leather couch taking up a whole wall by itself. Before she could stop them her thoughts turned towards the comforts of such a large couch. She couldn't stop an image of Dylan Matthews' long frame stretched out along the length of it. She managed to hold back the gasp of surprise at the quivering in her stomach. She pulled her gaze away from the couch and locked it on her folded hands. For the life of her she didn't know what was going on with her. But she suspected it had something to do with the eyes so steadily focused on her? Reluctantly she raised her gaze to meet his. There was such a heated look in those blue depths. Her nerves were frayed and her patience was near its end. Why didn't he say something? Anything dammit.

   Just then, he spoke and she wished he hadn't. His voice reminded her of her favorite brandy. Deep and smooth. It just kind of rolled over you and you didn't realize how strong it really was until it was too late. Sasha hoped he didn't have the same after affects of indulging in too much. While going down it was satiny smooth, but the next day she always woke up with a dreadful headache, a bad taste in her mouth and regrets. She spared a glance from beneath her lashes and fought the smile threatening to break free. She'd bet though just like her favorite drink, even with all the side effects, he knew how to keep a woman coming back for more. She just barely stopped the giggle that threatened to spill forth. She lifted her head to see if he had heard anything when she noticed him gazing at her with an expectant look. Oh god she could have crawled under his massive desk in embarrassment. Yep, just like a night of partaking of too much brandy. She couldn't recall what had happened and she wanted to die.

"I'm sorry. Did you ask me something?"

Great. Now she was blowing her chance at a good first impression. Or was she technically on her second impression since they'd already met earlier? Well kind of. Oh dammit. If she kept this up she may as well just pick up her briefcase and leave. Just save herself any further embarrassment. Though he tried to hide the smile by coughing and putting his hand in front of his mouth, she knew it was there. It was the way his eyes crinkled at the corners. Okay Sasha you have got to stop, she all but yelled at herself. This was so out of character for her. To be sitting in an interview for a job that was the culmination of what she'd worked so hard for over the past several years and to be blowing it.

"No apologies are necessary. I have been known from time to time to be caught unaware," he said clearing his throat.

He paused as if considering something before dismissing it.

"How about we start again?" he said standing up, his hand stretched out towards her.

"Dylan Matthews, chief financial officer for Presco Financial."

Was he serious? Even still wondering the reason, she found her hand reaching towards his.

"Sasha Jordan, future executive financial analyst of V.I.P. accounts for Presco Financial."

Warm fingers closed around her cold ones and Sasha realized she hadn't imagined the earlier jolt of electricity. She stared at their joined hands and took a deep breath of much needed air into her lungs.

"I like confidence in an employee."

He released her hand slowly before taking his seat once more.

"Now why don't you tell me why you should get the job?"

For the next hour she did just that. Her brain was still frazzled so she began with the basics. But it wasn't long before her natural charm and charisma came rushing to the forefront as she began to take control for what was probably the first time since she'd stepped into that elevator. And it felt good. As she answered each of his questions she began to feel more and more at ease. She relaxed in her chair, leaning back, her legs crossed at the knee. The tension between her shoulders began to lessen and the butterflies, which had invaded her stomach upon entering his office, retreated. She was on comfortable ground. Business she could handle. All the crazy emotions and feelings she'd been dealing with since her first chance meeting with Dylan Matthews was another story entirely. She didn't think she'd ever seen anyone look at her the way he did. It was as if he was privy to her most private thoughts and knew where her mind automatically went when she thought of him. Maybe it was just the way he looked at everyone. Perhaps in her own "badly in need of an ego boost" mind she had seen what she wanted to see. Catching the attention of a man like the one in front of her would be quite a coo. For someone else but definitely not her, she reminded herself. It wouldn't work for her because everything about the man went against her rules.

    Sasha tried to fight off the sudden feeling of disappointment that came over her. But in her many pitfalls with men, she had realized some years ago she had to come up with something to make the many mistakes she'd made in the past mean something. By paying attention to what she'd done wrong, she'd discovered certain situations could be avoided and the mistakes not repeated. So, she had come up with what she called her *"Rules for Love"*. They were five simple rules she had used for three years now to avoid being unnecessarily hurt by men who were all wrong for her. And rule number one was no dating outside her own race. It was nothing personal against men of other nationalities. She just figured dating was hard enough as it was without mixing colors and really confusing things. But there was something about this man, she couldn't deny, that made her want to break every one of her rules and that's what made him so dangerous to her.

Chapter 3

Dylan sat reviewing the notes he'd managed to make during the interview. He glanced at Mike's comments and felt satisfied he'd reached the right decision. During the interview he'd watched the woman in front of him relax and take control. The way she had conducted herself throughout the whole process provided him with glimpses of what a client would see when dealing with her. Her relaxed demeanor and smile would instantly put them at ease. The way she spoke in layman's terms when discussing her current responsibilities at her company told him she would be able to relate to someone who had never dealt with a financial analyst before and had no idea how one could benefit them. She would be able to explain precisely how she was going to help them. He sensed modesty, something not always thought of as an asset. He liked how she refrained from over glorifying any of what she had accomplished in such a short period of time with her current employer. Though in his opinion it was nothing short of impressive. He'd read the glowing letter of recommendation from her department manager and knew they hated to loose her but acknowledged she had outgrown their company. He had no doubts she would be an asset to Presco. The more he'd learned about her the more intrigued he'd become.

    Sasha Jordan was not the type of woman he normally went for. Dylan held onto the grunt at the back of his throat. He was glad she was different. For a while he'd thought himself incapable of attracting anything other than the shallow, self serving women he'd been known for dating over the past few years. It's one of the reasons he'd taken a much needed break from the social circuit he normally dwelled within. He'd gotten tired of the man eaters who often graced his arm at such functions. Only wanting him to ensure their faces showed up in the papers the next morning. He had to admit it was a life he was growing increasingly weary of. Glancing up at Sasha, who was sitting quietly in front of him a smile on her face, he realized he was ready for a change and she could quite possibly offer him that. She turned him on on so many levels. And he was glad to say it went deeper than looks. Sure she was a beauty on the outside and when she smiled her brown eyes sparkled but more than that she was intelligent. He cringed as he thought of some of the conversations he'd had or attempted to have with the women he had dated in the past. And there was no way he was going to just let her walk out of his office without at least trying to see where this attraction could take them.

The ringing of his phone broke into his thoughts. "Yes Carla," he replied tersely into the phone. His frown deepened as he listened to his secretary. "No it will have to wait. I'm already behind schedule and it's not that pressing of a matter," he replied.

He glanced up at Sasha an apologetic expression on his face. He saw her glance at her watch and took note of the way she was once again fidgeting in her chair. He could feel any connection he'd made during the interview quickly slipping away. He needed to make his move fast.

"Carla," he interrupted. "Just reschedule the video conference call for tomorrow after two o'clock. That should be fine."

That said Dylan hung up the phone. "I apologize for the interruption."

"No apology needed. I hadn't realized it was so late," she said checking her watch again. "I'm sure you had no intentions of being tied up this long."

He noticed the way she looked everywhere but at him. He knew he made her nervous. He only hoped it was a good nervous. The kind that spoke of mutual attraction and maybe an uncertainty of how the other felt. If that was the case he was about to make certain there were no doubts to where his thoughts and feelings were on the matter.

***

Sasha looked anywhere but at the man sitting across from her. The smile now gracing those full lips was too much for her. During the interview she'd been able to forget the crazy emotions he invoked as she'd gone about the business of convincing him why she was the only candidate for this job. But now her mind was no longer preoccupied with business and was free to wander to things better left alone. Like how there was a lock of hair that kept falling over his forehead and how the corners of his eyes crinkled in the cutest way when he looked to be deep in thought. And oh yeah, the fact he had the most amazing blue eyes she had ever seen. Yeah it was definitely time to leave.

"You make it sound like torture," Dylan replied, giving her a slanted grin.

It was the one from her dream earlier in the elevator. Wait when had she established she'd been dreaming?

"Trust me it was anything but. In fact I have enjoyed this far more than I could have anticipated. Presco is a company that firmly believes in promoting from within whenever possible. Unfortunately we were not able to do that this time and have been searching for just the right fit for this position for quite some time."

She could understand that. It was a position where Presco's multi million dollar customers were involved. The person for this job would be responsible for personal accounts and not company accounts. It was a whole different ballgame when it was your money on the line as opposed to a company's. So she nodded her head in complete understanding.

"When do you think a decision will be made?"

"Actually, I have made my decision," he paused briefly before continuing. "And the job is yours if you want it."

Sasha couldn't have kept the excited look from her face if she had wanted to. For weeks she'd fretted over whether or not she would hear anything on the resume she'd submitted on a whim. It had been four long months of waiting until finally she'd received the call for an initial interview. Then there had been more weeks of waiting until she'd gotten a second interview. The panel interview had followed. By the time she'd received notice of her interview with Mr. Shaunessy, she had been so weary of the whole process she'd almost withdrawn her name from the running. But now as she allowed the excitement of obtaining the job she'd wanted take over, she was glad she hadn't. There was nothing better than knowing a company as prominent as Presco found you worthy.

"Thank you very much Mr. Matthews. I would be honored to accept."

The discussion over salary and job responsibilities lasted another thirty minutes. Having done her research and knowing what she was worth to her current company, Sasha had figured she would be more valuable to her new one.

She was still riding high over Dylan's praise of her negotiation skills, when she felt rather than saw a change in the way he was regarding her. She brought her eyes to meet his slowly. Afraid and excited at the same time of what she would see reflected in their blue depth. It only took her a second to realize the gaze staring back at her no longer held an interest for Sasha Jordan, new employee of Presco Financial, but for Sasha Jordan the woman.

She watched as if in a trance as Dylan pushed back his chair and rose smoothly to his feet. She didn't have long to wait before his destination was clear. His lean body was perched on the corner of his massive desk with his legs crossed at the ankles. She kept her gaze firmly locked just below that magnificent chest of his, but just above his taut stomach which led to other areas of his anatomy best left unnoticed. Her palms grew damp and her pulse rate quickened at his nearness. Suddenly it was a struggle for her to get any air into her lungs.

"Now Sasha, if I may address you by your first name?" he asked pausing.

All she could manage was a small nod. Her eyes still locked on that small area she had deemed would not send her into cardiac arrest.

"Sasha," he said his voice coming out silky smooth.

The way he said it felt almost like a caress against her skin. For one wild moment, she allowed herself to wonder how it would sound if he were to call her name at the height of passion, just as an orgasm moved through him.

"I'd like to discuss another matter with you."

Sasha was certain she didn't want to know what it was he wanted to discuss. She knew it with every part of her being. But she sat just the same, unable to move, unable to breathe as she waited for him to continue.

"I normally don't make it a habit of hitting on people who work for me. Especially ones I've just hired."

A soft chuckle sounded from above her.

"In fact I can honestly say I have never dated anyone from within Presco. Just makes for better working conditions. But there is something about you. I find myself wanting to get to know you outside of the office."

All remaining air left her lungs. Oh god. What was she supposed to do now? Her insides screamed for her to say yes. They begged for her to give them what they'd wanted since first laying eyes on him in the elevator. She dragged a much needed breath of air into her deprived lungs in hopes it would allow her to think a little clearer.

She attempted to bring forth the good sense and reasoning that had served her through the years. She tried to convince herself it was not a good thing his being interested in her. But the only thing rushing to the forefront was excitement. Excitement over the fact a man like Dylan Matthews wanted to get to know her better. Joy of finally having confirmation she had not been imagining his earlier interest. Heat crept up her neck over the implications. If she hadn't dreamed it then that meant…. She slowly lifted her gaze to meet his. A wave of panic washed over her at what she saw. The intensity reflected in his gaze was enough to cause her to run screaming from his office or push him to the floor and have her way with him. This was not good. With great effort Sasha found her voice and prayed it wouldn't betray the chaos going on within her.

"Mr. Matthews," she began.

"Please call me Dylan," he interrupted throwing her another slanted grin.

Changing the Rules

Her will almost crumbled under the weight of that smile. She took another deep breath and tried again.

"Mr. Matthews I'm certain we will become better acquainted to some degree through my employment here. However, I would prefer we keep any relationship between us strictly professional."

A thoughtful look came across his face. Good, she told herself, he's thinking about this rationally. He was a numbers guy and would be able to deduce the futility of any personal relationship between them. Besides it was what was best for all involved if they kept things strictly professional. The sadness sitting in her chest over what she'd never know caught her a little off guard. Sasha quickly pushed it to the back. This was for the best.

"I don't believe I can do that. What's more I'm not positive that's what you really want either."

Dammit, she screamed inside. How could he possibly know what she wanted? They'd only just met today. Her mind conjured up an image of their ride up together earlier. The look she'd sent his way had definitely been one of interest, if not something more. But that had been a dream, she told herself. There was no way she could have been so bold as to ... Oh god she needed to make this right. And make him understand.

"Mr. Matthews I'm not sure what has given you the impression I would be interested in something other than the job I came here for this morning."

A deep chuckle met her ears and she cringed. "Sasha, surely you're not going to sit there and tell me you don't feel the electricity in the air around us. I felt it the moment I laid eyes on you. Even before you got in the elevator this morning."

Changing the Rules

Chapter 4

Sasha's head came up. It was confirmation she had hoped would never come. He had known she was looking at him. Reacting to him. How had he been able to remain so causal and relaxed when she'd practically been on fire? But he hadn't had he? He'd reached for her and she'd wanted his touch. Her face flamed with embarrassment. Her eyes fell to her proclaimed safe zone once again.

"That's right I recall every aspect of our ride up in the elevator this morning. How could I not?"

His voice had softened and the way his blue gaze roamed over her was affecting her breathing. The warmth of it spread through her body. Had he really been as affected by their encounter as she had? She wished she could tell herself it didn't matter but she found she wanted to know she held some mysterious power over him, as he seemed to have over her and her better judgment.

"It took every ounce of control I possessed not to push you against the wall and have my way with you."

Have his way with her? The thought both thrilled and frightened her at the same time. The question of whether or not she would have attempted to stop him crossed her mind. Oh god she was in way over her head. These types of things didn't happen to her. No matter how exciting it was to have a man the likes of Dylan Matthews express his interest in her she could not accept the offer. Nothing good could come out of it. Besides she didn't do white men and after her last go round of romance in the work place and the disaster it had turned out to be she had added that to her list of rules. Why did she need to keep reminding herself of these simple things? Sasha realized she needed to get out of here before she made a fool of herself for certain.

"Mr. Matthews I make it a habit to avoid office relationships and I'm sorry if I gave off confusing signals."

"It's Dylan and I don't think there was any confusion on my part about where your thoughts were earlier."

Finally he moved to take his seat behind his desk, his elbows on the surface. But his gaze was no less intense. How could she respond to that? She knew exactly what he was referring to. Think Sasha. This conversation is heading towards dangerous grounds. Grounds you are not familiar with. Who the hell was she kidding? She'd been on unfamiliar grounds since they finished discussing salary.

"Have you ever dated a woman of color before ….Dylan?" Sasha asked her tongue wrapping around his first name.

"I will admit I have not had the pleasure. But in case you hadn't noticed, I am trying to rectify that right now," he replied sending her another smile.

Flattery was not the emotion she should be feeling and Sasha knew that. But as much as she hated to admit it, she was elated he had never dated a black woman before. It meant he found her interesting enough to be the first. She tried to tamp down on the feelings as best she could. She needed to concentrate on finding a way out of this mess.

"Well then there you have it. I believe what we might have here is just the thrill of a new experience."

Now there was a thought that didn't exactly thrill her. She wanted to feel as if she were different to him. Not another reasonably attractive black woman he was hitting on. Sure Sasha realized that wasn't the point but she couldn't help it.

"Ah but I would have to disagree with you. I don't exactly live in a bubble. I've had ample opportunity to date a woman of color. But with any woman I have to be interested enough to want to make a move," he said leaning forward on his desk, his gaze holding hers captive. "And you, Sasha Jordan, from the moment I first saw you rushing across the lobby have been moving me in one direction. And that direction is closer to you."

She had dealt with gorgeous men before. Men who seemed to exude sex from their very pores but she had always been able to control her feelings and think rationally. But with Dylan, she found it hard to control the pure, hot, unexplainable desire that moved through her. She had never had this emotional tug of war within herself before. Fighting against what her body wanted without caring what the cost and what her mind said she could never have.

"Let me ask you a question? Have you ever dated someone outside of your race before?"

Was he kidding?

"Never," she said as if he'd dealt her a serious insult.

Apparently her response hadn't offended him if the small smile on his lips was anything to go by.

"Then I can understand your reluctance to do so. All I'm asking is for you to think about it. Think about what we could possibly offer one another in a relationship."

"And what is that?" she snapped.

Changing the Rules

She recalled another relationship that was to have been about a mutual sharing but had backfired royally with her on the other end looking like a fool. It was the reason she didn't get involved with anyone she worked with.

"A helping hand up the corporate ladder as long as I grace your sheets. I refuse to have people wonder how I got this position. Questioning which set of qualifications you used to hire me."

Sasha saw the muscle in Dylan's jaw twitching and wondered if perhaps she'd said too much. Thoughts of her ex, Melvin, had caused her words to come out harsher than intended. Her hopes for her perfect job were quickly going down the drain.

"That's not what I was getting at. If you give me the chance you will find I guard my personal life very closely and those who share in it even closer."

She wasn't sure how to respond so she simply sat there in silence for several moments. How had this interview gotten so far off track?

"I believe it's time for me to go Mr. Matthews."

Sasha picked up her briefcase and stood. She allowed the rational side of her brain to take over as she squared her shoulders and locked her emotions away deep inside. Later she would pull them all out and sort through the muck to find out what had happened. Once she discovered what had happened she would be able to ensure it never happened again. Maybe add a new rule. Rule #6: No drooling over guys in elevators - they may be your interviewer and future boss. The thought brought a small smile to her lips.

Dylan brushed past her, successfully blocking her way to the door. He was so close. The fragrance of his cologne wrapped itself around them like a cocoon. She was sure he could tell how much he was affecting her. How could she hide it? It was in the rapid rise and fall of her breasts beneath her jacket. It was in the wide-eyed expression she now held as she stared at his chest.

"So it's running for you. Strange you struck me as braver than that." He challenged.

"I'm sorry but you have me confused with someone else. Just ask my friends. I'm not very brave at all."

She fought the urge to push him out of the way and walk out the door leaving him and the job she had dreamed of obtaining behind. She was certain the reality of this would hit her as soon as she got out of this office and could think clearly again. But Sasha wasn't sure if she would feel anger over her complete loss of control over the situation or with herself for not taking him up on what he was offering.

"Where exactly should I go to ask them?" Dylan asked nonchalantly.

"Murphy's Bar and Grill."

She could have bitten her tongue off. How could she have been so thoughtless as to divulge such personal information? Had she subconsciously wanted him to know where he could find her if he wanted to see her again? No, that was definitely not it. Just calm down, she told herself. After all it's not like he will ever show up there. Surely he had better things to do than try and track you down at a hole in the wall like Murphy's.

He surprised her when he stepped aside without commenting. Her gaze reluctantly followed him as he moved to the window behind his desk. Sasha took his turned back as her cue to leave. She headed towards the door once more. Well so much for her perfect job.

"Someone from our human resources department will be in touch with a starting date."

"Excuse me," she asked turning around to face him. She was surprised to find herself facing his back still.

He glanced over his shoulder an amused look on his face.

"Yes Sasha a start date. Despite anything else, you are still the most qualified applicant for the position. That is if you still want it."

The challenge was clearly written in his gaze.

"Of course I do but I don't want there to be any confusion about what I'm accepting. I am accepting the job with Presco Financial. I am not interested in pursuing any relationship with you other than the professional one my job dictates."

Her heart hammered against the wall of her chest as she waited barely breathing for his response.

"Naturally, I look forward to any professional relationship that might grow between us. I'm sure it will be a most fulfilling one. However, allow there to be no misunderstanding on my part. What I am after from you is strictly personal."

She was about to comment when he held up a hand.

"I believe for all your protests you feel this thing between us just as I do, but for whatever reason you don't want to acknowledge it. Denying it doesn't make it any less true."

He fixed her with a look that left no doubts this was far from over. A thrill ran up her spine. She decided to question it's meaning later when she was alone and could think clearly.

"Allow me to be the first to say, congratulations on the job Ms. Jordan. I'm sure I'll be seeing you around," he said turning back towards the window before she could see the full smile now gracing his face.

Changing the Rules

Sasha didn't say another word, simply turned and walked out the door, closing it softly behind her. She headed towards the elevator and then rushed across the lobby floor. It seemed an eternity since she'd walked across its massive marble layout.

Once outside, she took huge gulps of air to calm her frazzled nerves. The parking lot, which had seemed to take forever to get across earlier, now seemed like nothing. She fumbled in her purse to find her keys when she saw her car. Finally, having located them, she pushed the button to unlock her doors and practically fell into the seat. She leaned her head back against the headrest. She was emotionally drained. She could still see the determination on his face. The intensity in those blue eyes. She tried to stop the excitement racing through her veins.

She ran her fingers through her braids in an attempt to push thoughts of Dylan Matthews from her mind. But it was no use he was seared into her brain. What was she going to do now? She'd gotten the job of her dreams. But what about the man who seemed determined to be apart of her benefits package?

Chapter 5

As promised, someone from the human resources department called Sasha the day after the strangest interview she had ever had with a start date. It allowed for a thirty day notice. She hadn't needed it though. Her boss had been aware of her chances of obtaining the job with Presco so the number of projects she was in charge of had drastically decreased so she had been able to begin her new job two weeks sooner than expected. She had just finished her second week and was out celebrating with her best friends, a month after her first encounter with Dylan Matthews. She hadn't told any of them about that day. As she sat sipping her brandy, pretending to be interested in the conversations going on around her, she was glad she'd decided to keep the encounter to herself. For all of Dylan's big words he hadn't made any attempts to contact her. And it wasn't as if he didn't know where she was. The first morning she'd seen him, she'd braced herself for the encounter. She'd felt confusion over her odd feelings. On the one hand she had hoped he would ignore her presence and continue his conversation but on the other she'd wanted him to immediately excuse himself and come over to greet her. A grunt of irritation passed her lips. She gave an exaggerated cough to cover it when eyes turned in her direction. Waving off their concern she took another swallow of her drink and nearly choked in earnest this time. Served her right for being so damned hypocritical. He'd kept on with his conversations as if he hadn't even seen her. She'd told herself with each passing day she was glad he hadn't sought her out. It was the way she wanted it. Maybe he'd finally come to his senses and realized there could never be anything between them except a working relationship. It was funny how that thought depressed her as much now as it did each time she'd said it over the last two weeks. She couldn't possibly have been giving serious thought about a relationship with him. Could she? Sasha shook off the crazy thought. Of course not. She who preached religiously to her friend Cat about dating outside of ones race. Now there was someone who had no hang ups about dating a white man. Or any other color of man for that matter. There was someone she could introduce Dylan to if he wanted to try a black woman. Her hand paused midway to her drink. Sasha was sure she should have found the thought amusing, but somewhere she must have lost her sense of humor.

She was still deep in thought when the back of her neck began to tingle. She got the distinct impression someone was watching her. Turning in her chair, her brown gaze scanned the crowd of people around her, not really knowing who she was looking for but knowing who she'd like to find. Murphy's was crowded tonight even for a Friday. But as her gaze continued to scan the crowd she didn't notice anyone looking in her direction. What had she expected? That a chief financial officer of a major financial institution would have nothing better to do on a Friday night than show up here? If he wasn't interested enough to see her at the office where it was convenient he sure as hell wouldn't go out of his way to come to a little out of the way bar. A few minutes later the feeling returned but she didn't turn around this time. What was the use?

"Hey earth to Sasha. Are you still with us here?" Cat called out from her seat directly across from her.

Sasha looked up from where she'd been staring into the bottom of her glass to find four pairs of eyes all staring at her. She felt her face heat. She had been so deep in thought she hadn't even noticed she had become the center of attention.

"Of course, I'm still here. Where else would I be?" She replied forcing a smile to her lips.

Changing the Rules

If she didn't get out of this funk soon she would have a lot of explaining to do. As much as she loved her friends they could smell a problem a mile away and wouldn't relent until they got to the bottom of whatever was going on. This was one thing she was determined to keep to herself.

"Oh I don't know. Maybe off in lala land with your next door neighbor," Cat said wiggling her eyebrows up and down, a wide smile on her face.

Everybody laughed including Sasha. Aw irony, she thought taking another sip of her drink. For five long months she had been concentrating her efforts, and those of her friends, on getting her neighbor to notice her. He was after all the type of man she went for.

Louis Wainwright was a successful attorney and was your classic tall, dark and handsome black man who appeared to be headed in the right direction. It looked like their efforts were finally paying off. They'd been talking almost every night for the past three weeks and Louis had finally asked her out a few days ago. Sasha knew she should be overjoyed. She'd put some serious time into that man. And he was after all the type of man every black woman hoped to find and marry. After their conversations, she knew Louis had his mind headed in the direction of the alter within the next two years. It was a direction she'd like to move towards herself. Only after getting to know him a little better she didn't know if she wanted to move in that direction with him. Louis was from a good old southern home in Alabama where his mother never worked outside the house who had raised nine kids. So his old fashioned ideas of a woman's place didn't really sit well with her. Oh he was accepting enough of a wife who worked, at least until the babies started coming along. Then he fully expected her to stay at home going forward. Sasha could almost wrap her mind around the concept but could she really see spending the rest of her life with a man who was only happy when talking about the law? She had endured countless lawyer jokes and lingo which would have meant nothing to her had she not had a fascination with the mystery channel and an old southern lawyer with a bad gray suit from Atlanta, Georgia. All of those things combined with the fact he bored her to tears had made for really long nights on the phone. She refused to allow herself to admit there was another reason for her sudden lack of interest. She refused to even entertain the thought of it.

    "Naw I'm actually good right here. Thanks," she finally replied.

    "Then what's your deal? You have an awesome new job and the professed man of your dreams is finally taking notice. You should be dancing on top of the tables. But you're sitting there like a bump on a log," Cat said, a look of concern in her brown gaze. "What's going on?"

How could she tell them everything that was going on with her? Oh she was sure Cat would love nothing better than to hear she was no longer interested in Louis. She'd never been too impressed with him anyway. What had she called him? A pompous ass with no social skills. She'd come to that conclusion after only one conversation with him at a neighborhood function last year. But she would definitely want to know what had brought about the sudden change. As would all of her friends. And that was something she wanted to keep to herself.

"I know. I guess I just have a lot on my mind," she said shaking her head and smiling as she recalled all the other things Cat had said about Louis. She hadn't found them funny at the time, but they were quite amusing now.

"A lot of what on your mind or should we be saying who?" Safari Lawson asked from the other end of the table and everyone laughed.

Sasha simply smiled and hunched her shoulders. Relief filled her when her friends resumed their conversations, thankfully taking the attention off of her.

"Did something happen at work? Something you want to talk about?" Cat asked having moved beside her,

her voice was lowered to prevent anyone else at the table from hearing.

She noted the serious expression now displayed on her friend's face and knew she had to find a way out of this funk. One concerned friend she could possibly put off, but four. There wasn't a chance in hell with those odds. She loved her friends dearly and they'd seen each other through some pretty rough times. Sasha knew she could tell them anything. But would they understand what was going on? Hell, she wasn't even sure she understood it herself. And in reality what was there to talk about? She refused to believe if Dylan had been serious about pursuing her that he wouldn't have found a reason, made up or real, to contact her. No matter what she said. The Jerk.

"It's nothing like that. I guess I'm a bit overwhelmed with everything that's been going on."

At least it wasn't a complete lie. She was definitely overwhelmed. Overwhelmed by the amount of time she spent thinking about Dylan Matthews. Overwhelmed by the number of times she had dreamed about him in four weeks. And definitely overwhelmed by the need she felt to see him.

"Ok, so how is the new job going?"

"It's great. And the people are really nice," she answered smiling, grateful for the change of conversation.

"Good," Cat said looking around. "So how long are we gonna be here before we blow this place to go dancing? But don't let me rush you. This is your party after all."

Sasha laughed at the expression on her friend's face.

"It doesn't matter to me. Let's get a group consensus. Hey," she called to the rest of the group, "what time are we gonna be leaving for the club? I know B.J.'s got an early showing in the morning so she can't be out late."

She smiled over at her sister, who sent her a look of thanks for remembering. Their friend, Lynn Saunders, answered. "I say we give it about another hour or so. Is that ok with everybody?" She asked checking for nods around the table.

"Well then I believe this calls for another round of drinks," Cat said looking around for their waitress. Her eyes grew wide when the waitress stepped up to their table with their order already on her tray.

"What's this?" she asked the waitress.

"A gentleman at the bar has bought your next round of drinks," the waitress said putting them on the table.

Sasha's stomach grew queasy. She told herself to stop being silly. It couldn't be him. Not here. It was someone else. It had to be. But still she couldn't keep a glimmer of hope from springing forth.

It was Cat, the non-stop flirt, who responded.

"Well, I guess we should do the nice thing and at least thank him."

She rose from the table, pulling down her unbelievably short mini skirt and followed the waitress.

As Sasha watched her go she sent up a silent prayer that it was anyone but Dylan. Cat had never met a sexy man she didn't like and Dylan Matthews was dripping sexy from every pore. And he was just her type. Male.

Chapter 6

Dylan smiled as he watched Sasha from across the room. He had managed to not only locate Murphy's Bar & Grill but had been coming here for the last couple of weeks since his interview with her. In the beginning it had been with the sole purpose of a chance meeting. Despite the fact he hadn't had any luck until tonight, he had kept coming back. He'd even brought a few friends with him. It was different from the normal places they went to unwind. He didn't have to worry about the social climbers who typically went with that type of environment nor the annoying flash of a camera in his face at every turn of his head. It was a much welcome change. He liked the laid back atmosphere and the food was excellent. But tonight was what he had been waiting for. He'd been sitting at the opposite end of the bar, nursing a beer, when she had walked in with a group of women. He'd sat and plotted his move all night but hadn't come up with anything that wouldn't have him sounding like a bad pick up line. Then a stroke of luck had come his way. The waitress serving their table had stepped over to the bar to place a drink order. He had wondered what a woman like Sasha would drink. Then his opening had hit him. He had immediately motioned the waitress over. He had explained to her he wanted to order a round of drinks for a specific table. His most winning smile combined with a very healthy tip had gotten him the assistance he'd been looking for. Out of curiosity he had asked what they were drinking and instantly knew the brandy was Sasha's. Smooth and dark, apparently how she liked her men. But he was about to change all of that. Before he was done she would be trading in that snifter of brandy for a sophisticated and palette pleasing white wine.

Dylan was still congratulating himself on his actions when he felt a presence behind him. Yes, he thought to himself fighting the urge to pump the air with his fist. He turned around slowly and barely managed to hang onto the smile on his lips. Though he recognized the woman standing in front of him as one of the women at Sasha's table it was not the one he'd been hoping for. But he had noticed this one as well when the group had come in. The woman in front of him appeared to be in her mid to late twenties with shoulder length black hair with hints of what looked like burgundy running through it. Her complexion was lighter than Sasha's and she had the most intriguing smile. As he looked closer he saw she only had one dimple, making her appear mischievous. Or was the glint of humor in her brown eyes the reason. Whatever it was he liked her instantly.

"Hello. It's my understanding we owe our round of drinks to you?"

The woman in front of him asked. A smile played around the corners of her mouth as she glanced from him to the chair beside him. Dylan, feeling a little embarrassed at his lack of manners, motioned for her to take the seat beside him. As she sat down in the chair, he noticed the graceful way she moved. The directness of the gaze slowly taking him in and the confident way she had approached him. This woman was very much used to the game men and women played. While she continued her silent perusal, he glanced past her shoulder to where Sasha sat at their table, her back still to him. Tonight she had her hair down allowing her braids to flow past her practically bare shoulders. When he'd seen her walk in wearing the flowing sundress that had barely come to her knees it had set his blood on fire. As she'd gotten closer he'd noticed the deep v of the bodice. There was no way she could be wearing a bra with an outfit like that. His dick had come immediately to life. It had taken everything in his power not to walk up to her and throw her over his shoulder like some damn caveman and storm out of the bar.

"You know it's rude to be gazing longingly at another woman while in the presence of one. Especially one who's not used to being ignored by a man."

He wasn't sure what he expected to find when he turned his attention back to her, but he wasn't prepared for the gleam of amusement in her eyes. The women he normally dealt with would either have been pouting by now over his lack of attention or spitting daggers at him. Either way it would have made for an impossible situation. But the woman in front of him seemed not a bit concerned.

"My apologies I hope I didn't offend you."

She tilted her head to the side and looked at him again. He saw the intelligence flashing in her eyes and a slow smile spread across her face.

"No apology needed. So who's got your attention since it's obviously not me," she said a soft chuckle escaping her lips.

His smile widened. Yeah he definitely liked her. How would she react if he told her it was her friend he'd been practically drooling over? Would her smile vanish? Better to keep his cards close to his chest for now.

"No one in particular," he said flashing her a huge smile meant to put her off the scent of how close she was to the truth.

She paused as if in thought for just a moment.

"Hmm, is that right? Funny I would have thought you were trying to impress someone or at the very least gain their attention. You did after all just send an eighty dollar round of drinks to a table of black women you don't know. Or do you?"

That dimple was back and the gleam in her eyes said pure mischief. Dylan shook his head. Had he been that obvious or was this woman just that damned astute? He got the impression it was the latter. He bet not much got pass this one.

"Okay I'm busted. I didn't just randomly pick your table out of all the others," he said a sheepish look on his face.

"Now we're getting somewhere. So, who are you? And why are you drooling over one of my friends?" she asked leaning back in her chair. Her look said she fully expected him to explain himself.

"You see there's a very good reason for that. I work with her."

At her raised eyebrow, he remembered she'd been at the table with several females.

"I work with Sasha," he clarified.

"Okay that takes care of which friend. Now how about the who are you part?"

Though she maintained a relaxed posture in the chair, Dylan saw a wariness come into her eyes. He liked that she was protective of her friends.

"Dylan Matthews," he said extending his hand to shake hers. "And you are?"

Dylan didn't miss the look of recognition that flashed through her eyes at the mention of his name. He wondered what reference she recalled his name mentioned. For his sake he hoped it was something good.

"Caitlyn McPherson," she said shaking his hand.

She had a firm grip.

"Well it's nice to meet you Caitlyn."

"So what's the deal with you and Sasha?"

Suspicion laced her voice and the wariness in her gaze hadn't changed. Even though he now felt as if he were under a microscope, he liked her straightforwardness.

"Honestly?" he asked.

Her look answered the question better than any words could have. He found himself liking her even more.

"Nothing is the deal with Sasha and me. But I'd like to change that if I can. As a matter of fact, I'd like for there to be lots between us."

***

Cat just sat there staring at Dylan Matthews as if he'd just grown three heads. She'd thought she recognized him as soon as he'd turned around. The disappointment she'd seen flash across his face before his smile had returned served only to peak her curiosity of why a man like him would be in Murphy's ordering drinks for a group of black women. Well she guessed she had her answer now.

Sasha had caught the eye of a man who had been declared one of Chicago's Most Eligible Bachelors, for the last three years, and she hadn't told any of them. No wonder she was spaced out tonight. Hell if any man could make a girl rethink some things it had to be the one sitting across from her.

Of all of their friends Sasha had always given her the most grief over her dating habits. Now look at her. She was mooning over a white man. She covered her mouth to try and stop the giggle but it refused to be contained. Before she knew it she was laughing in earnest. Tears rolled down her cheeks. She reached for a napkin to wipe them away. It was a good thing she hadn't bothered with mascara tonight. The inane thought made her laugh harder.

When she noticed Dylan frowning Cat made a real effort to stop, but every time she thought of Sasha with a white man she felt the giggles bubble up again.

"I'm sorry," she said trying to catch her breath. "But you have to know Sasha to know how funny this is."

A look of determination entered Dylan's blue gaze. Here was a man on a mission. Any further laughter died in her throat.

"Ok," she said clearing her throat and straightening in her chair. "You're determined, I can see that. But if I were to say to you that you have no chance in hell of getting her to even consider anything personal, you would say what to me?"

His gaze hardened for just a moment. Alrighty then, Cat thought. She liked him. And maybe just maybe it could work.

"Okay I can see you're serious about this," she said holding up her hand when he opened his mouth to speak.

Decisions. Decisions. To meddle or not to meddle that is the question.

"Listen I'm sure you're used to dealing with a certain kind of woman," she began.

"You're not gonna pull that never dated a black woman card are you," Dylan asked.

Cat paused.

"Excuse me."

He gave a deep exhale of breath.

"Look no I have never dated a black woman before. No I am not just looking for a new experience. And no, any other black woman will not do," he said a bored expression on his face.

"You've obviously addressed this whole thing with Sasha huh."

"Yes and it didn't go well to put it mildly," Dylan said running his hand down his face. A sign of weariness and frustration.

"I can probably tell you why."

She paused again. Once she began there was no going back. If she confided in this man and things didn't end up well, her bond with Sasha could be damaged beyond repair. She glanced over at her friend. It didn't take her as long as she thought it would to make up her mind. If there was anyone in need of saving from themselves it was Sasha.

"You see Sasha has these rules for dating. A list she calls her *"Rules for Love"* and she takes it very seriously. In fact for her to even consider anything with you would break her number one rule. No dating outside her race," she said glancing at him to see his reaction. A smile played around the corners of his mouth.

"You're kidding me right?"

"Nope unfortunately not. There are a few that might give you some problems, just in case the first one isn't big enough. Like rule number five, no breaking any of these rules no matter how gorgeous the guy. So the way I figure it you're kinda in a catch 22. You're white and you're gorgeous."

"This is a joke isn't it? There is no way a sane and rational woman like Sasha could hope to abide by those rules. She'd have to be living in a bubble somewhere," Dylan said disbelief clearly written on his face.

Cat grunted her agreement.

"That's only two of the five rules. You don't get a break with any of the others either. For example, rule number two – no mixing business with pleasure. Rule number three might give you a problem as well, but that's only if you can get pass rules number one, two and five. No casual sex," she said on a whisper.

You're not laughing now are you, she thought as she took in Dylan's wide eyed expression.

"What's number four? No kissing outside on your front porch if there's a full moon?" he asked, a sarcastic twist to his lips.

"Close but no cigar. It's no believing in fairy tales."

Cat sat back in her chair, her legs crossed at the knee and waited. She couldn't begin to imagine what he must be thinking. In her opinion he should get a date just for not running straight for the hills after hearing all five of those stupid ass rules. She shook her head as she recalled how many times she'd been regaled with them after yet another of Sasha's relationships had ended. She could have told her why they never worked out. Her friend had the very bad habit of always going for the wrong guy and she put way too much thought into it all. Prime example Louis, the snooze from next door. Who said if you were a black woman you had to limit your choices to only black men? The way she figured it you had just cut your options for finding a good man by a good seventy percent.

    Feeling his gaze upon her, Cat lifted her eyes to meet Dylan's. A frown was creasing his brow but to his credit he was still sitting there. She saw the determined gleam was back within his blue gaze. His jaw was set. She'd shocked him but he was back on his feet. A smile took shape on her lips. Yeah she liked this one.

Chapter 7

Dylan shot a quick glance over at Sasha. What the hell was he about to get himself into? Or had he already gotten into because try as he might to deny it he was in for the long haul. Anything else was not an option. And apparently she was more complex than even he'd originally thought. Either that or she was crazy as hell. And further more what did it say about his own sanity to be considering moving forward in his efforts to woo her?

"I'm not sure whether or not I should thank you for telling me why my chances are slim to none or not. In hindsight I think I would have preferred to remain in the dark."

"What and continue to think you were loosing your knack with the women? No I couldn't do that to you."

He tried to return her smile with one of his own but it didn't quite make it. His brain still challenged the logic of the decision his body had made the instant Sasha had stepped onto that elevator a month ago.

Changing the Rules

"So I guess you'll just have to continue to drool from afar."

The question was clear. She wanted to know what he was going to do. Once more he found himself glancing in Sasha's direction. The back of her head greeted him same as it had all evening. What he wouldn't have given for her to turn in his direction and give him a smile. Some kind of sign his efforts were not in vein. That he hadn't imagined the connection between them. But as much as he willed it she didn't turn.

"You know when I interviewed Sasha I had no idea..."

Dylan paused when he noticed the surprised look on Cat's face.

"When you interviewed Sasha? I thought her interview was with Michael Shaunessy, not the big money guy at Presco. Or did you get demoted and that failed to make the front page of the Chicago Tribune?"

Dylan's loud bark of laughter had people turning in their direction. He didn't even question how she knew of Michael Shaunessy or of his position with Presco. He'd pegged her as intelligent from the moment he'd turned to find her there and the longer he spoke to her the more she proved his point.

"Uh no. I have not been demoted. I am still CFO or the big money man of Presco as you put it. And I took over Sasha's interview at the last minute when Michael got called away."

"Okay time out," she said making the sign with her hands.

"So you interviewed Sasha, she got the job. And then what? At some point between then and now you addressed your interest in her. And you got the whole *I don't do office relationships* lecture or the *I don't date white men sermon*."

Oh she knew her friend well.

"Actually, I had the great pleasure of being on the receiving end of both of those."

Cat laughed.

"I'm not surprised. Sasha doesn't do very well when faced with things outside of her comfort zone. And I would have to say that you Mr. Matthews are way outside her comfort zone."

"So she hasn't said anything about me at all, eh? I don't know how much more of this my ego can take," he said putting on a pained expression for her benefit.

"Then maybe you should consider another woman. I'm pretty sure her intention when she left your office was to forget all about you. But I would hazard a guess to say you've been on her mind." At Dylan's raised eyebrow she explained.

"She's been a little preoccupied lately. We all just assumed it was due to her neigh... her new job. But now I have to think it could be you."

A look of disbelief passed across his face.

"She made her feelings pretty clear about not wanting to have anything outside of business between us."

"Damn, that must have been some interview," Cat said laughing again.

"Let's just say it wasn't your everyday run of the mill variety."

He laughed himself as he recalled certain details of that day. The elevator scene had begun showing up in his dreams with a different ending each time. Though they all had something in common, he always got the girl.

"You were saying something about Sasha's mood and she might be thinking about me. How can you be sure it's me and not some other guy? Like perhaps this neighbor of hers?" Dylan asked with a wink, letting her know he had caught her faux pas from earlier.

She laughed good naturedly at being caught.

"I wouldn't worry too much about him if I were you," she said with a dismissive wave of her hand. "You've got tons more personality than he does. Not to mention you're much better looking. And besides I like you."

Her words gave his spirits a much needed boost. He wondered if all of Sasha's friends were this cool.

"So you really want to do this?"

He knew exactly what she was asking him.

"Caitlyn, when I first met Sasha I felt something I haven't felt in a long time towards a woman, a genuine interest in getting to know her better. And I know she felt something too, she's just too stubborn to admit it. All I want is the opportunity to explore what we might have together. If it doesn't work out then it wasn't meant to be. But I just want the chance to find out."

He ran his fingers through his hair and allowed his attention to be distracted by what was going on around him. He couldn't believe he'd just laid himself bare for this woman. How far the mighty had fallen? He never would have guessed that when he found a woman he really wanted to get to know it would be this difficult. Dylan glanced back in time to see a slow smile spread across his new friend's face. Sure enough he had been correct in his initial assessment. She only had one dimple.

"My friends call me Cat," she said smiling at him and stuck her hand out again.

His relief was unequaled and he gratefully accepted her hand and her help. Dylan lifted her hand to his lips and brushed a light kiss on the back of it, smiling his thanks. Things were definitely looking up.

***

Sasha's heart stopped beating for a moment and her eyes got big as saucers. She jerked her gaze away from the scene and felt an odd sensation in the area of her heart. She fought the urge to rub her chest as the tingling spread. She didn't want to examine what she was feeling. Well, she had been right after all. Dylan was definitely Cat's type.

Chapter 8

"Sasha Jordan."

"Ms. Jordan, Mr. Matthews would like to see you in his office at eleven forty-five," came the no nonsense voice of Dylan's secretary, Carla, on the other end of the phone line.

It was more like a command than a request.

"Do you know what it's regarding?"

She didn't think anything she was currently working on required a meeting with the CFO of the company. Not to mention the fact she really didn't want to see him. Liar her body replied. Despite the way things had turned out on Friday she had still gone home and had the most erotic dreams of him. She'd woke Saturday morning feeling guilty. Had she and Cat ever lusted after the same guy before? Hmph doubtful.

"No I do not. Just make sure you're on time. Mr. Matthews hates tardiness."

The line went dead.

"Yes sir."

Changing the Rules

Leaning back in her chair she tried to think of any reason he would need to see her in his office. When she'd seen him in the coffee shop this morning as normal she had braced herself for the encounter. After all he and one of her best friends had made plenty nice on Friday night. She was certain he would approach her but she had been wrong. He had gotten his coffee quietly and left. Now that she thought back on it he looked to be deep in thought. Probably still thinking on the events of Friday night, she thought pushing herself to her feet. It sure as hell hadn't been far from her mind for the rest of the weekend. Once Cat had returned to the table they had left shortly after that for the club. The only thing she'd wanted to do at that point was go home but she'd done her best to act as if nothing was out of sorts with her. In doing so she'd over indulged and had a helluva hangover on Saturday. One so severe she didn't fully come back to herself until Sunday. But even that had not been enough to stop the damn dreams. Pacing back and forth in front of her window, the thought of what Dylan could want continued to plague her. Certainly he couldn't be calling her in to talk about Cat.

"No way," she said to her empty office.

That would be just plain tacky.

Thirty minutes later, on her way to Dylan's office, she was still pondering the same issue. Memories of her first meeting with him, assailed her as she exited on his floor from the elevator. Sure she'd walked away that day with her dream job in hand but Dylan had offered her something more. He'd offered her an opportunity to step outside of her normal and for the first time she had actually wanted to accept the offer. But thank goodness her common sense had prevailed. Common sense or fear, a little voice questioned.

Seeing the desk outside his office empty, Sasha wondered where his watch dog was. She supposed it wasn't a fair statement but every time she saw Carla she reminded her more and more of a bull dog. And did the woman have something against smiling. Maybe she didn't have any teeth. That brought a giggle from her. When she glanced at her watch and saw she was now five minutes late for her meeting, all laughter died. Dammit she hated being late. Tapping her foot in agitation she glanced at the closed door to Dylan's office. Maybe he was in there waiting for her. Her steps faltered as she moved towards the door. Taking a deep breath she knocked softly.

"Come in," came the reply from the other side.

Dylan sat behind his massive desk, his head bent.

"Carla has Ms. Jordan arrived yet?"

"Yes I have."

She tried to hide her pleasure at the look of shock on his face. But her smile wavered some at the slow once over he was now giving her as well as the smile lifting the corners of those full lips.

"Well good morning Sasha. You're late," he said coming around the desk to greet her.

She shifted uncomfortably at his steady gaze.

"I was waiting outside. Carla wasn't there so I wasn't sure if I should come on in or not."

He motioned for her to take a seat in one of the chairs in front of his desk. To her surprise instead of returning to his place behind the desk he took the chair beside her.

"My door is always open for you. I want you to know that."

Intense blue eyes stared at her. Not wanting him to see how uncomfortable he was making her she lowered her gaze.

"I'm sure you feel that way about all of your employees."

A small laugh sounded beside her but she refused to look. She knew what his smile could do to her insides.

"If it makes you feel better to think that then go right ahead."

Not sure of how to respond she remained quiet. Dylan made her feel and think about things she had no right to think about. Especially now since all evidence proved he was obviously planning on hooking up with Cat if he hadn't already.

"What did you want to see me about Mr. Matthews," she asked hoping her voice didn't sound as breathless to him as it did to her.

"I thought we had already discussed this Mr. Matthews business and decided you would call me Dylan, Sasha," he said moving his chair a little closer to hers.

The temperature in the room increased by a hundred degrees with each inch closer he got. The scent of his cologne drifted in her direction. She breathed deep against her will. A deep sigh of pleasure lodged itself at the back of her throat. How could the mere smell of a man get her so excited?

"Mr. Matthews what we agreed was that there was going to be nothing but business between us."

"No I distinctly recall advising you of something very different. I think you and I could have something special together. Can't you feel it?"

Her gaze was drawn to the hand now covering hers. She stared at the difference in their coloring. Instead of it looking completely out of place as she'd hoped, it looked good against her skin and God knows it felt heavenly. Such a simple touch was causing so much havoc with her senses. Had any man's touch ever affected her like this before? If the feel of his hand on hers did this to her she wondered how many pieces she would explode into if he touched the rest of her. Wait. This was all wrong. She should be thinking of a way to escape his touch not how she could get him to touch her in more places.

"Dylan if you didn't have anything business related you wanted to discuss I think I should be getting back to my office. I have some work to get done before the end of the day," Sasha said but made no move to get up from her chair nor did she move his hand from hers.

The hand over hers began caressing up and down her arm and her stomach tightened in response. The slow movement was causing heat to spiral through her body and pool in the pit of her stomach. Dear God. Was this a test of some kind? She prayed for the strength to make it through.

"I understand if you have work to do," he said his hand slowly moving up her arm to caress her shoulder. "I seem to have fallen a little behind lately myself. You see I can't get a certain pint size woman off my mind long enough to concentrate on anything other than how to get her in my bed. Do you have any ideas that may help?"

In his bed? Her mind went black before a very clear image of them together in her bed came to mind. Her heart threatened to beat out of her chest.

"No? Well I had a few thoughts of my own. Perhaps you can help me test them out. Just to see if they would be effective or if I should go back to the drawing board."

He rose smoothly from his chair and moved behind her. Sasha held her breath not knowing what he was going to do but she didn't have the courage to turn around and look. When his hands began working the tension from the taut muscles in her shoulders a low moan escaped before she could stop it. Oh god she was in deep now. She should have left when she realized he hadn't wanted to discuss anything business related, but she hadn't. She'd stayed knowing things could possibly turn in this direction. Had she wanted them to? Had she wanted another chance at what she'd turned down a month ago? No her brain screamed, but her body merely grunted under the pleasure of his touch. Her head rolled back on her shoulders and her eyes drifted closed. It felt so good and she was so tense and tired from fighting with herself. A deep sigh escaped when she felt his warm breath close to her ear moments before warm lips surrounded her lobe and drew it into his hot depth. A shiver ran up her spine as he gently tugged on the small gold hoop secured there. She knew she needed to stop this, but her willpower seemed to have taken a vacation. She tried to call upon some feeling of being harassed but she found she liked Dylan's form of harassment. The more he drew on her ear lobe, the tighter the knot in the pit of her stomach. Her breasts grew heavy with need. Her nipples hardened into painful peaks against the soft material of her bra. It was as if he had heard the call of her body when his hands wandered down her front to caress her breasts. Pleasure shot through her. There was no way she could hold back the groan that came from her. Moisture flooded her panties. The more he pulled and tugged on her nipples the greater the throbbing between her legs became.

"Dylan," Sasha moaned.

"Yes," he said his lips grazing against her slender neck.

"I don't …"

She paused when he nipped the delicate skin before smoothing over the mark with his tongue.

"You were saying sweetheart?" he questioned gently against her ear.

It took a moment for her to get her thoughts together and even then they were filled with the blue eyed devil playing havoc with her senses and her body. What had she been saying? She had to wonder about the importance of it when his hands returned to her breasts. He rolled her engorged nipples between his fingers. Even through the material of her blouse it felt like heaven. The thought brushed her mind of what it would feel like if they were bare before him. She might not survive it.

"Oh god Sasha I want you so much," he breathed against her. "Can't you feel it? This thing that's between us."

She wanted to scream at him that she felt it. But… her mind was struggling to regain control.

"I don't think this is a good idea," she said clawing her way to the surface through the fog of desire he was wrapping her within.

"Do you always think about everything?" he asked moving around her, making sure to brush his hardened body against her.

Opening her eyes to see what he was about to do next she found herself getting lost in his gaze. When he reached down to help her stand electricity shot up her arm to her breasts. Her already hardened nipples throbbed painfully.

"Did you feel that?"

He lifted their joined hands for her to see. All Sasha could do was nod. She didn't trust her voice not to betray how she was feeling and how close to the edge she was. If he led her to that big couch against the wall she didn't know if she would have the will power to stop him or if she even wanted to. Her breath held in her throat as he began to walk, pulling her along where their hands were joined. When they stopped she glanced up. Confusion and disappointment filled her. They were not in front of the couch which sat on the other side of the room but in front of the closed door to his office.

"Do you still think there's nothing between us?" he asked placing his fingers beneath her chin to bring her gaze to meet the storm brewing in his blue depths.

What could she say? She had been ready to allow him to do god knows what to her. Feeling embarrassed over what could have happened she pulled away from his gentle touch and lowered her head.

Dylan's arms enclosed her in their strong embrace. He refused to budge as she struggled against him. When her nipples began to throb caused from the friction of her movements, she stood still as stone. She almost moved again though when she became aware of the growing bulge against her stomach. He was huge. Images of what it would be like to have him laying atop her filled her head. If he was as big as she thought would he fit. Her body yelled at her to find out. Now. It was almost her undoing when Dylan's fingers began thrusting through her hair. When had it come down. She had put it up as normal into a tight bun at the back of her neck. He must have done that when he was…. Sasha stopped those thoughts dead in their tracks. Any thought of what had happened was likely to have her dragging his ass to the couch instead.

"It's okay. I don't understand what's going on between us either or why it's happening. All I know is that it is and I don't want to fight it," he said and kissed her temple with such sweetness.

She closed her eyes against the tenderness. It felt so good to be held in his arms. Then memories of Friday night came back to haunt her and his tenderness towards another caused her to come crashing down out of the clouds she'd been flying in just moments ago. She pushed herself out of his arms and was reaching for the door when it unexpectedly swung open. Sasha made an awkward lunge to get out of the way to avoid being hit. Her attempts brought her hard against Dylan's massive chest. He closed his arms around her small frame to keep her from falling. Her already sensitive breasts rubbed roughly against him as she tried to right herself in his arms. The heat from his body combined with the scent of his cologne threatened to take her back where she'd been just moments ago. On the precipice of surrendering. She opened her eyes and found herself staring into brilliant blue eyes filled with desire that had never truly disappeared. Surely his gaze was a reflection of her own. Heat spread from her chest which was pressed tightly against his to the lower half of her body, which was throbbing to the fast paced beating of her heart.

"Pardon me. I didn't see you there," Carla said, stepping further into the office, her eyes widening in apparent surprise at the sight of Sasha in Dylan's arms.

Sasha realizing how things must have looked quickly stepped away from Dylan as if suddenly burned by the touch of his skin against hers.

"It was my fault. I was just leaving," she said and walked through the door not looking back.

She headed down the hall to the elevator. She couldn't believe what had just happened. It was exactly what she'd wanted to avoid. A scandal at work was sure to happen. Even if it had been innocent and Carla's coming through the door had been the cause of it. Sasha was sure when the rumor mill got hold of the incident it would have turned into her being on top of him on his desk or something else just as preposterous. As thoughts of the potential fall out continued to plague her, she couldn't help but recall other aspects. Like how her breasts had felt as they'd been pressed against his rock hard body. How his hands had cupped their heavy weight as he'd nibbled on her neck. She looked at her hands as she punched the button for her floor and noticed the slight tremble. She couldn't deny the desire still running through her veins. Stepping off the elevator onto her floor, Sasha let out a huge sigh of frustration. This is why she tried to always live within the rules she'd set up. To keep her out of situations like this. Maybe she should have given Dylan a copy of those rules so he would know how impossible anything between them was. Closing her office door behind her, she didn't think it would matter. She got the distinct impression Dylan Matthews played by his own set of rules.

Chapter 9

Sasha leaned heavily against her closed front door and breathed a huge sigh of relief. She kicked her shoes off and undid the buttons of her suit jacket. It was good to be home. It had been a long stressful week at work thus far and she still had one more day to go.

Three days had passed since the incident in Dylan's office and she had heard nothing of it yet. She'd been holding her breath all week long. Every time she walked by people talking she steeled herself against the possibilities they were talking about her. But no one appeared to be looking at her differently. She wasn't sure what to think of it but she was glad she wasn't the new talk of the company. That kind of recognition she could do without. She still hadn't decided what to make of Dylan's actions or her own responses. And how did Cat fit into all of this? It didn't make any sense. She had never thought she and Cat had the same taste in men. Most of the men she was attracted to Cat openly admitted not to be her type in any way. And vice versa. But this was different. What had changed? As if you don't know, her rational mind told her.

Not wanting to go down that road or admit the all too obvious answer, she pushed herself away from the door and headed upstairs to change clothes. She glanced back at her shoes and briefcase and decided to retrieve them later. She had just walked into her bedroom when the phone rang. Her hand hesitated. What if it was Cat? Guilt and shame washed over her. She pushed them down as best she could. She had been unconsciously avoiding her all week. It was just that she was so confused and hadn't decided how to handle things yet.

"Yeah right," she grumbled to herself catching the phone before it could go to the answering machine.

"Hello."

"Hello Sasha?"

Her world stopped. She wished it had been Cat on the other end.

"I hope I didn't catch you at a bad time."

Tell him he did. Tell him you were just on your way out. Say anything to get him off the phone now.

"How did you get my phone number?"

Anything but that, her brain yelled. It had been the first thing to come to mind.

Deep male laughter sounded in her ear.

"I have access to all the personnel records."

"Oh," she said feeling silly for asking such an obvious question.

"Are you busy?"

Here's your chance again, her brain yelled. Get him off the phone now. If you want to talk to a man, call Louis. He is still waiting for us to call him back from last week.

"No, I'm just getting home."

Oh god it's hopeless now. Then all went quiet in her head. She breathed a mental sigh of relief.

"Working late again?"

What did he mean by that? Again. How did he know what kind of hours she was keeping? Did he have people watching her?

"Yes if you must know. I was given a new client and I'm working on a tight deadline."

"I heard. According to Shaunessy you're handling it quite well."

A frown appeared between her eyebrows.

"Have you been checking up on me?"

Sasha was positive he could hear the accusation in her voice.

Another deep chuckle came across the phone lines.

"I would prefer to think of it as confirming what I already knew."

"And what exactly would that be?" she asked suspiciously.

"That you would be an asset to Presco," he replied simply and so matter of fact.

"And when did you figure that out? Monday in your office?"

Instantly she wished the words back in. Had she really wanted to bring up Monday's incident? There was no denying it had been weighing heavy on her mind for several reasons. She tried to tell herself it was because she'd been walking around on pins and needles uncertain if her reputation at Presco would be over before it had even had an opportunity to grow. But no longer could she ignore the real reason. Her feelings were hurt. Plain and simple. He hadn't bothered to contact her after Monday. No note, no messages. No random calls into his office. Nothing. She'd been bouncing back and forth between feeling hurt and angry for three days now. Not only over his actions but over her own as well. Then her confusion over where Cat could possibly fit into things had only made matters worse.

A deep sigh came across the phone lines.

"No, but since you've brought it up, that is what I wanted to talk to you about," he said.

What was that odd note in his voice?

"What about it?"

Her insides churned. Did he regret his actions? How awkward would that be? Because when she closed her eyes she could still feel his hands cupping her breasts and pinching her nipples. Could still remember how badly she'd wanted him to strip her bare. How she had wanted his hands on her bare skin. It had plagued her all week as to why he had stopped? Hadn't he known she was too far gone to put up much of a fight? Or was it a different reason entirely. Had he begun thinking of Cat? Her stomach churned for a whole different reason at the possibility. She'd brushed upon it before but had pushed it to the back of her thoughts each time. She didn't want him to think of anyone but her when they were together. Wait no that's not right. She didn't want him to think of her at all. Feeling as confused as ever she fell backwards on the bed. She rubbed two fingers to her aching temple.

"I wanted to apologize for what happened on Monday," Dylan began.

She sat up. He did regret what had happened. She was surprised at how that little bit of information hurt.

"I had wanted to speak with you about it earlier, but this week has been one straight from the pits of hell. Even now I hate doing this over the phone. But when I stopped by your office I discovered you had already left."

She was glad she had left when she did. Sasha didn't think she could have dealt with him explaining to her all the reasons why he regretted his actions on Monday. She knew she shouldn't care because it was better this way and she knew it. But her feelings had been manifesting since the day she'd first laid eyes on him. No matter what she tried she hadn't been able to successfully exorcise him from her thoughts. He obviously wasn't having the same problems.

"No, this is fine," she said quietly. "I can imagine you've been busy."

"Yes well even still there's no excuse for my allowing almost the entire week to pass before I contacted you. I know how sensitive you are about things like this."

Sasha didn't know what to say. She didn't want him to apologize. She didn't want to hear about how he regretted touching her. And she sure as hell didn't want to hear the reason for that regret was Cat.

"Look Dylan, Mr. Matthews. It's not necessary for you to apologize. We can pretend what happened never happened. So if that's all you were calling for, allow me to reassure you it's as good as forgotten."

She hoped the gods wouldn't decide to strike her down for the outright lie she'd just told. His touch was forever seared into her brain. And her body.

"I think maybe you misunderstand me Sasha. I'm not calling to apologize for what occurred on Monday. Quite the contrary. I have no intentions of forgetting it and would like to see what I can do to ensure it happens again. I was apologizing for Carla's interruption and any embarrassment it caused you."

He didn't regret what happened? He wanted it to happen again? She tried to fight the smile. This was insane. One minute she was telling herself it was good he wanted to forget everything that happened. The next here she was like a giddy little teenager who's just been told the captain of the football team liked her and wanted to go steady.

"I want to also assure you I have spoken with Carla and not one word of what occurred in my office will go beyond my office."

Something in his tone gave her the impression he'd done more than just speak with his secretary. But that was fine. Whatever means he thought necessary to keep her name out of the gossip mills.

"Thank you for that. I have been worried."

Feeling suddenly better, she pushed herself off the bed. There was no need in lying to herself about the reason so she opted not to think on it at all. She moved to her dresser, which sat along the back wall of her closet to find something to put on.

"I figured as much. I'm sorry again for that. But I want you to know it is not my intentions for anything we have to be sullied by gossip. I will always do my best to protect you from that."

The sincerity in his voice touched a spot deep inside. She wanted desperately to believe him. To trust in what he was saying. But how could she realistically trust someone who was making the moves on her and her best friend at the same time. Suddenly she had to know. She needed to know if there was truly anything between him and Cat. If there was, then no matter what her feelings on the situation she would be happy for her friend and she'd stay away from him at all costs. But she had to know one way or the other.

"How much longer are you going to be in the office?"

She glanced at her watch. It was almost nine o'clock. Could he be waiting for Cat to get off from work? She often worked late during the week to cut down on her take home workload over the weekend and her office was only minutes from Presco. There was a depressing thought if she'd ever had one.

"I'd be willing to leave right now if you said you wanted me to come to your place."

Oh god did she ever. She wanted him to come so he could make her cum. Sasha turned the thought over in her head and realized she'd meant it. She took a deep breath and realized she could no longer avoid the issue at hand.

"Can I ask you something," she said before she lost her nerve.

"I can be there in twenty to thirty minutes depending on how far you live from the office. Hell I'll run the risk of a ticket to make it sooner," he said a slightly amused tone to his voice.

Need raced through her fast and hard. How long had it been since a man had shown this much interest in her? How long since her body had reacted like this towards one? Her ex, Melvin, had never been able to get the reaction from her sexually he'd wanted. At the time she had thought there was something wrong with her and had seriously considered seeking counseling of some kind. Now as she stood in the middle of her closet, she had to wonder. Maybe it hadn't been her after all because Dylan seemed to be able to get her blood pumping alright.

"That's not what I wanted to ask you. I wanted to talk about …," Sasha began.

What was she going to say? How was she going to ask the first man in forever to make her panties damp, if he had the hots for her best friend? Hell how could she not?

The questions surrounding what she'd seen on Friday night had driven her slowly insane since. She'd avoided Cat like the plague for fear she wouldn't be able to act normal with her. Sasha knew she would not jeopardize her friendship with Cat over a man. Not even Dylan Matthews.

"You wanted to talk about what Sasha?" Dylan asked.

His voice had dropped several levels and came out soft and husky. She almost groaned at the pleasure of the sound.

"I wanted to talk about Cat."

Soft laughter met her ears. What the hell was so funny? In fact this was as serious as serious could get. Her temper flared.

"What about her?" he asked on a laugh.

"Well for starters you can tell me if you want to fuck her."

Chapter 10

Dylan fought hard to hold onto his laughter. The word "fuck" sounded so unnatural coming from Sasha's lovely little mouth. But he'd be damned if it hadn't made him hard. Well, harder if that were possible, he corrected. He'd been throbbing with need since she answered the damn phone.

"You had better not be laughing at me Dylan Matthews. There is nothing amusing about this situation."

Says who? He found it funny as hell. He'd spoken to Cat a couple of times this week. She'd told him Sasha had seemed to be avoiding her phone calls since the night they'd met. Cat believed Sasha was under the impression they'd started something. But after her reaction in his office on Monday, he hadn't been too sure. She really did know her friend. Hell it had even been Cat's crazy idea to call Sasha to his office to see what kind of reaction he could get from her and see how far he could push things. That encounter had almost pushed him to push her to the leather couch in his office.

"I would never dream of laughing at you Sasha," he said, the corners of his mouth quirking with his efforts to keep his face and tone of voice serious.

"Whatever. You didn't answer my question."

No he hadn't. Feeling an evil streak a mile long he decided to prolong things just a bit. After all she'd put him through hell since their first meeting. *But what if she's not asking for the reasons you want?* Dylan immediately dismissed the thought. No. He refused to believe anyone who responded the way she had in his office had no feelings for him at all.

Glancing down at the papers strewn across his desk and then at the clock on the corner of his desk, he realized he may as well pack it up for the night. Any hopes of concentrating any further on the reports he'd been looking at were a wash now for sure.

"Hmmm, I didn't," he commented absently packing what he needed into his briefcase.

"You know perfectly well you didn't. And if you do want to, you know with Cat, then how could you have done what you did on Monday with me?"

Laughter almost got the better of him once more, but he managed to contain himself. Oh she was fit to be tied now. The normally calm and collected analyst was all woman now with feelings muddling up the waters. Good he thought. He grabbed his suit jacket off the coat rack and locked his office. He headed down the back corridor to the private elevator that would take him to the private parking garage assigned to executives of the company. Once the elevator doors swooshed open he stepped inside.

"Do you really think so poorly of me that you would believe I could be interested in Cat and then turn around and make out with you on Monday?"

Silence was his only answer. He realized he was more than a little insulted. She had so little faith him in. He wondered if that was all men or if it was just him.

He leaned heavily against the elevator wall and thought back to his first encounter with Sasha. The soft sighing woman from the elevator had made a partial reappearance in his office on Monday. Enough to bring his blood to boil. It had been the reason he'd stopped when she'd asked him to. Dylan had realized if he'd kept touching her, he'd have taken her right there in his office. That would have been decidedly more difficult to explain away to an avid gossiper like Carla. A frown appeared as he thought back on his conversation with his secretary. He'd thought to simply explain the situation to her. Make her see her barging into his office had created the awkward moment. But when he'd stepped outside his office she had been on the phone with one of the girls in Michael Shaunessy's office and his blood had immediately hit boiling point. The thought of it being a legitimate conversation had never occurred to him. All he could think about was Sasha's name being tainted. When he'd called her name she had practically jumped out of her chair. An evil smile appeared on his lips as he thought back on it. The guilty look upon her face had said it all. Any thoughts she may have entertained about sharing what she had seen in his office were quickly dispelled the moment he'd opened his mouth. Her very job was on the line and he'd made sure she knew it in no uncertain terms. As she'd gotten up to leave, he'd also made sure to remind her to knock before entering his office in the future.

"I guess I have my answer don't I," he said in reply to her silence.

Stepping from the elevator he headed for his car. He wasn't surprised to see it was one of the few remaining. A last minute meeting to discuss the new company in California they had just acquired explained the presence of several others. Luckily he had been excused from that meeting. But considering the number of problems that were surfacing with financial reports he didn't know if his luck would hold out.

Changing the Rules

He got in his car and reached for his blue tooth earpiece before placing his phone in its cradle. He rarely used the damn thing but his mind was on other things and the last thing he needed was to be handling a cell phone while trying to navigate downtown Chicago traffic. Even at this late hour there never seemed to be a good time to drive downtown. He sat with both hands on the steering wheel and listened to the tense silence coming from the other end. He gave an exasperated sigh. Was he simply kidding himself where Sasha was concerned?

"You don't know how much I want to believe differently," she finally said. Her response so soft he almost missed it.

"Then why don't you. Besides what would give you the impression I want to sleep with Cat? Hell I only just met her last week."

Another pause came across the phone lines. He was growing weary of this. He thrust agitated fingers through his thick hair. Maybe he should rethink this after all. Cat had told him it would be difficult and he'd assured her he was up for the challenge but now he wasn't so sure.

"I saw you two on Friday night. You kissed her."

There was something in her voice that pulled at his heart. He thought back on the night and didn't recall kissing Cat. Had he and not even realized it? It could have happened and he just didn't remember. They'd gotten so comfortable during the time they'd spent talking. He could have given her a peck on the cheek when they parted. But he was positive there hadn't been any passionate kissing going on. Maybe Sasha had been looking at someone else and merely thought it was him and Cat.

"If I did then I assure you it was no more than a friendly little peck on the cheek. Surely nothing to give you the impression I wanted to sleep with her."

He continued to wrack his brain at what she could have seen or thought she had seen.

"It was the hand," came the soft reply.

He couldn't have heard her correctly.

"I'm sorry what?"

A deep sigh met his ears.

"I said it was on the hand."

What the hell? It was starting to annoy him Cat being right about so many things. This took jumping to conclusions to a whole new level.

"You mean to tell me you came to the conclusion I wanted to fuck your friend, who I had just met, from my kissing her on the hand?"

It sounded ridiculous. He knew she could clearly hear the amusement in his voice and didn't care. This was insane. She sure had jumping to conclusion down to a science.

"No I got it from the fact you kissed her hand and I know Cat. We've been best friends since forever and when she sets her eyes on a hot guy it's all over but the fucking."

He couldn't help it. He leaned his head back against his head rest and laughed out loud. He was falling for a head case. A woman that could be truly certifiable.

"You're laughing at me again," Sasha said.

"You're damned right I am. I don't know who to be more insulted for myself or Cat. Does she know you hold her in such high regards?"

Somehow Dylan got the impression Cat wouldn't be insulted. As a matter of fact he could see her shrugging it off.

"Cat knows I love her. But you still didn't answer my question."

"Oh for pete's sake Sasha. No, I don't want to fuck Cat. In case I haven't exactly been making myself clear I'd like to fuck you."

He cringed as the crude words left his mouth. Dammit.

"Sasha I'm sorry that didn't come out right," he said quickly.

He didn't get an answer. He looked down at his cell phone and saw the connection was still open. Okay so she hadn't hung up on him.

"Sasha?"

Great. Now he'd really done it. She wasn't even talking to him. Why the hell hadn't he held onto his temper better?

"Did you mean that," she asked quietly.

"Of course. It was rude of me to say that."

A soft laugh sounded.

"No not that. Did you mean what you said about wanting to you know …"

Dylan stopped breathing. He licked his suddenly parched lips. What should he say? Should he admit it was all he'd thought of since their first meeting? Should he spout some relationship correct bullshit about waiting until she was ready?

"Yes," he managed to croak out pass his clogged throat.

There was another brief pause on the line.

"Good," she said and hung up.

"What the hell?" he asked looking at his cell phone.

What the hell had just happened? She'd asked if he wanted to fuck Cat. He'd come back with the Neanderthal comment about wanting to fuck her and she'd said … good.

Changing the Rules

Dylan ran his fingers through his hair in stunned confusion not sure of what would happen next or what his next move should be. He gave a deep sigh as he started his car and pulled out of the underground garage. He had come to the decision a long time ago he would never understand women. And he had been okay with that. But he found himself wishing for just a quick glimpse inside the lovely head of Sasha Jordan.

***

"Matthews who are you waiting for?"

He focused in closer to get a better view of what Dylan Matthews was doing. He'd come off the private elevator a few minutes ago and now he was just sitting in his car on his cell phone.

"Who are you talking to my friend? Is it that blonde hottie from a few months ago from that art gallery opening or is it the blonde from the opera?"

Matthews had always had a thing for tall leggy blondes. For a minute he'd expected to see a woman walking off the elevator and head for his car. That would have been an unexpected move but he'd take it at this point. Though Matthews had always shunned away from pissing where he ate, maybe the woman was really hot and he couldn't hold back. Wouldn't that be something? So he had sat there and waited. But nothing. Matthews had stayed on the phone the whole time.

In his profession, you learned to read a person's face and body language. Sure he might not have been able to hear what was being said but he'd been able to get the jest of it. Something wasn't going as Matthews had planned. Amusement had started it off, and then he'd gone to being annoyed. That had only lasted a few minutes before his face had relaxed and he'd been laughing like a fool. Just before he'd left the garage he'd moved instantly between the "I fucked up" expression and utter confusion. All of that equated to one thing.

"You've got yourself a new woman don't you Matthews?" he said watching him finally drive off.

He put away his gear and drove out of the garage. Tipping the night attendant a fifty for letting him in, he headed for downtown Chicago. There were a few other spots he wanted to hit before he called it a night.

Excitement moved through him and the craving for a cigarette almost had him stopping at a local convenience store. Instead he reached on the seat beside him and pulled out a piece of that gum all the experts said would help. As he allowed the gum to work its magic, he couldn't help but wonder which one of the brainless blonde bimbos from the right side of the tracks had caught Dylan Matthews' eye this time. Not that it mattered. He'd be right there to give her what she was really after. Her face plastered all over the Chicago society pages.

Chapter 11

Sasha found herself lying on her back staring up at the ceiling unable to sleep. Dammit what was wrong with her? She'd slept little this week as thoughts of any possible fall out from Monday had plagued her. She should be exhausted. And her body was, but her brain refused to rest. Thoughts of Dylan and their brief conversation kept running through her mind.

She couldn't deny the pleasure she'd felt over his not being interested in Cat, but what did it mean for her. Was she really contemplating getting involved with him? Could she really do this? What about all those nights of preaching to Cat about her color choice in men? What about her rules? Dating Dylan would mean breaking every one of them. So what if her friends thought they were a joke. They'd kept her from making the same mistakes over and over again. But what if the mistake she was making now was ignoring what was there between her and Dylan?

She couldn't deny the fact that no other man had ever affected her like this.

She groaned in frustration and glanced over at the clock on the nightstand. Two-thirty. She reached for her phone and scrolled through her caller id. If his number wasn't there then it wasn't meant to be and she would move on. When she found what she was looking for, she paused. Her heart was pounding in her chest as she pushed the recall button.

Ring … ring…

What if no one answered? Should she leave a message? What if …

"Hello," Dylan answered sounding surprisingly awake.

Sasha hesitated. Okay now what, she asked herself. This is why she didn't act on impulses. She'd never been any good at it.

"Hello?" called the voice again.

"Hi. Did I wake you?"

"No I couldn't sleep and found myself lying here contemplating counting sheep. But I'd much rather talk to you."

Warmth spread through her body.

"I couldn't sleep either."

"Anything you'd like to share."

Share? There was no way she could tell him the real reason she was wide awake at this time of the morning, or could she.

"I ...um...I was thinking about your call. Well actually I was thinking about you after your call and that's why I couldn't sleep."

She cringed at the way she was stuttering and stammering. She was an intelligent woman and thus should be capable of putting more than two words together at a time. She threw her arm over her eyes and felt her face heat with embarrassment. Oh god. She should have just rolled over and tried counting sheep herself.

"I must say that comes as a surprise especially given the way you've been denying any attraction to me whatsoever. But I will admit I definitely find the thought pleasing."

"Just because I didn't admit it doesn't mean it wasn't there. Besides I thought you were interested in Cat," she responded settling a little further under the covers.

"Ahh yes, the infamous kiss on the hand. I can see where you could have gotten the impression we were hooking up," he said laughing.

Her insides quivered. She could listen to him laugh all night. Well not if he was going to continue to laugh at her.

Changing the Rules

"Okay I believe we've already been down this road. There's no need to revisit it," she said cringing when he laughed louder.

"Fair enough. What road would you like to travel now Sasha," he asked. All hints of laughter gone.

There was only one path she wanted to take with him. She was tired of fighting her attraction to him. And there was no denying he caused her to react in ways she never had before. Yet still she hesitated. Was it the whole black white thing that was bothering her so much? Searching deep, she didn't think that was it. Inter-racial relationships were more the norm than the exception today and where there would be some who turned up their noses there would be more people who didn't bat an eye. Was it his position at the company? She felt as if she were getting warmer. Dating a fellow co-worker had not gone well at all the last time she'd done it. But this was different. Dylan was no ordinary co-worker. He was for all intents and purposes her boss. And the last thing she wanted was for anyone to believe she was receiving preferential treatment because she was sleeping with him. Her stomach fluttered at the thought. Sasha stopped listening to all the arguments going on in her head and decided to listen to her body for a change. The deep seated need that had begun the moment she'd glanced over to see him leaning so casually against the elevator wall took center stage. She was tired of fighting against what she wanted and God help her, what her body was demanding.

"I think we should see where this takes us," she said hoping she sounded more confident than she was feeling at the moment.

There was no mistaking Dylan's sharp indrawn breath from the other end. She had shocked him and possibly herself in the process.

"Would you like to have dinner at my house? Tonight?"

"I would love to. What time?"

Relief washed over her at his acceptance.

"How about seven o'clock? We could do later if you're working late."

"No I will definitely be leaving the office on time. Seven sounds great to me. I'll bring the wine."

"Will you be coming from the office? I need to give you directions."

For the first time in weeks, she felt at peace.

"It'll probably be easier especially if you live close to the office. I live in Gurnee," he said naming an upper crust suburb surrounding Chicago.

"I live about thirty minutes from the office in Waukegan. So let me give you directions from the office."

"Okay hang on," Dylan said.

When he came back to the phone she gave him directions.

"Okay I got it. I'm looking forward to dinner Sasha," he said his voice soft.

A smile lifted her lips up. She realized she was too.

"So am I Dylan. G'night," she said and hung up.

Sasha lay for a minute just staring into space waiting for the nagging doubts over her actions to come. Surprisingly they didn't. She smiled into the dark room and took a deep breath. She felt good about her date. But what about Cat? Her smile faded. Sure Dylan wasn't interested in Cat but was she interested in him.

"Dammit why was nothing ever simple," she said into the dark room.

There was no way she was going to get any sleep tonight until she made sure things were going to be okay between her and Cat especially if she began seeing Dylan on a regular basis. A shiver of excitement raced through her. Cat had to be happy for her about this, she thought reaching for the phone one more time. She just had to be.

"Hello," the sleepy voice on the other end of the line answered.

"I'm sorry to wake you up but I need to talk to you."

She almost laughed at Cat's deep sigh. She could just imagine why Cat thought she was calling.

"Just for the record, there will come a time when I will be able to call you in the wee hours of the morning and harass you like this," Cat grumbled.

Sasha smiled. She couldn't wait for the day a man got Caitlyn McPherson all tied in knots. She wanted a front row seat for that one.

"Well I wanted to tell you I have a date for tonight," she said.

It was a good thing no one could see the huge grin on her face. They'd think she was nuts. But she couldn't help it. She was excited and she wanted to share that excitement with someone. She wanted to share it with Cat and she wanted Cat to be happy for her.

"I would say it's about time. He only asked you out two weeks ago. I don't know what took you so long to say yes."

Sasha giggled. She couldn't help it. It just came out.

"My date's not with Louis."

There was a pause on the line. This time she covered her mouth so her giggle wouldn't escape. It wasn't often she got the opportunity to catch her always on top of it friend off guard.

"Then who is it with?"

Changing the Rules

Her smile faded a little. Oh god here comes the hard part, she thought. What if she wasn't happy for her? What if she had planned to go after Dylan for herself? Well she can't have him because he's mine. Sasha was startled by how strongly she felt about the situation. It kind of caught her off guard but she didn't feel any remorse for it.

"It's with my boss. No, well he's kind of my boss. He's the CFO of Presco," she said stumbling over her words. She took a deep breath to calm herself down and tried again. "It's with Dylan Matthews the guy from the bar on Friday night. The one who bought our table a round of drinks."

She held her breath while she waited for Cat to say something. The silence was almost deafening. She found it odd that calling Dylan and asking him over for dinner had not been as hard as this was turning out to be.

"Cat are you still there?"

She checked her phone to make sure the connection was still there.

"Yeah I'm still here. So let me get this straight. You're no longer interested in your neighbor what's his name? Eugene? Malcolm? Boring?"

Sasha laughed through the nerves. Cat had never been terribly impressed with Louis and hadn't hesitated in telling her so. But to her credit she had continued to offer advice on what to do to get him to notice her.

"His name is Louis and no I'm no longer interested in him," she said humor lacing her voice.

Another pause.

"And we're not talking about a business dinner of some kind are we. Because business dinners don't count," Cat questioned further.

"No it's not a business dinner. It's a real honest to god date."

Bit by bit her giddiness was returning. Sasha covered her mouth with her hand to keep from laughing out loud. She had no idea where all of this was coming from. She hadn't had any of these crazy unexplainable urges when Louis had asked her out. But just knowing she had a date with Dylan made her want to get up and dance about screaming it over and over from the top of her lungs.

"So what do you think?" she asked cautiously holding her breath and sending up a silent prayer at the same time.

"Well, I think that if you had to go white you sure as hell picked a nice place to start. Dylan Matthews is hot," Cat said.

That was her undoing. All the giddiness broke free from her and it wasn't long before she and Cat were both laughing hysterically. She had Cat's blessings. Sasha wondered how her other friends would take it. How would her sister, B.J., react? The thought threatened to rob her of her good mood but she pushed it back. There would be time to worry about that later.

Chapter 12

"Hi," Sasha said opening the door for Dylan. He was right on time.

She noticed he'd changed from the suit she'd seen him in earlier at the office into a pair of tan khakis with a baby blue button down shirt. The color of his shirt really made his eyes stand out. Did this man look gorgeous in everything he wore?

"Hi," he said handing her the wine.

"You may need to put that in the fridge. It was chilled when I left work, but it took me a little longer to get here. Traffic," he said in way of explanation.

"That's okay. We can have it after dinner. Are you ready to eat?"

At his nod, she led him down the short hall to the kitchen, which was set at the back of the house. The kitchen was bright with an eat-in area. The family room was directly off of it, allowing for easy conversation between the two rooms. There was a formal dining room which she rarely used and had no intentions of using tonight either.

Dinner was a pleasant enough affair with conversation being light between them. They talked about a little of everything. From their childhood to how they came to be in their current careers. They also discovered a mutual love of jazz, rainy days and having a lazy Sunday every now and then. But all through the conversation the sexual tension was evident. It hung in the air between them like a combustible substance ready to ignite at any moment. Sasha had thought she would go up in flames a few times during dinner when they'd both reached for a roll at the same time. Tingles of pleasure had moved through her where their hands had touched. And the way his eyes had glazed over when he'd watched her lick sauce from the corner of her mouth had caused a responding groan of pleasure to become lodged at the back of her throat.

Once dinner was over she stood and began clearing the table. To her surprise Dylan rose as well. With a dirty dish in each hand, he walked to the sink and began running water. She stood watching him, her mouth slightly ajar, as he rolled up his sleeves. He turned the water off and glanced at her over his shoulder.

"You gonna bring me the dishes or you want me to come get them," he asked with a lopsided grin.

Her breath caught in her throat. He looked way too sexy with his sleeves now rolled up to his elbows and his hands covered in soapsuds.

"No I'll bring them to you," she said smiling like an idiot.

Once the dishes were done and the kitchen was clean she turned to him once more.

"Since we didn't get to have it with dinner would you like some wine now. I think it should be chilled. If not I think I can offer you a choice of something else."

She walked over to the refrigerator and peered inside to take stock of its contents.

"I have bottled water, soda, beer? If you'd like something a little stronger I think we have some left over stuff from the last time the girls were here."

Sasha waited for his reply but none came. Instead she felt his warm hard body pressed against her back.

"What I want can't be found in the refrigerator," he said licking her earlobe.

Her stomach clinched in arousal. She stood up and leaned back against him. The cool air from the refrigerator against her front contrasted with the heat against her back. She stepped back, surprised he allowed her enough room to close the refrigerator door, but Sasha quickly found herself sandwiched between the hard cool form of the refrigerator and the heat of Dylan's hard body.

She licked suddenly dry lips before she answered.

"And what is it that you want Mr. Matthews?"

Dylan cupped her small breasts and squeezed. She was barely able to contain the groan at the back of her throat.

"Do you have to ask Ms. Jordan? You make me hotter than I've ever been. And now I have you just where I want you," he said licking down the side of her neck to her shoulder where she felt his teeth grazing her skin.

A shiver ran through her body. Dylan stepped back and turned her around to face him. The same desire running rampant through her body was reflected in his gaze. She moved her hands up his massive chest to circle his neck.

"Sasha," Dylan breathed her name softly before lowering his head to hers.

Nothing could have prepared her for the first touch of his mouth on hers. The instant their lips met, she felt the shock waves run through her body. Sasha leaned in closer to the heat of his body while his hand cupped the back of her head as he deepened the kiss. Her mouth opened to allow him full access. She lost herself in pleasure when his tongue slowly licked hers. So soft was his touch, as if he were baiting her – daring her to join him in play. Uncertain, her tongue moved cautiously at first to touch his and her universe shifted. Her body felt on fire and he was the only one who could douse the flames.

Finally, he lifted his head, allowing them both to take a much needed breath. His forehead rested against hers as he ran his fingers through her hair. She sighed at the pleasure of his massaging touch on her scalp. So pleasant was the place she was in Sasha didn't want to ruin it by opening her eyes and allowing the reality of the situation to rush in. She was hooked on Dylan Matthews. Any illusions she'd tried to wrap herself in were quickly disappearing the longer she remained wrapped in his arms. She raised her gaze to meet his eyes and was almost gone again by what she saw reflected there. He was feeling it too. All she could think about was how short a trip it would be to her bedroom upstairs and how good it would feel to have the full weight of his body covering her smaller one. But was she really ready for that? Not wanting him to know how at odds she was, she lowered her gaze to stare at his chest. She was so confused. She didn't know what she wanted any longer. No, that wasn't true. She knew what she wanted but it contradicted everything she knew. Things had been so simple before she had met Dylan and she wanted that simplicity back. But would it really ever be the same now that she'd tasted him?

"I think it's time for you to go."

She spoke softly, her eyes still fixed on his chest. She didn't want to see the look on his face for fear it would be her undoing. His hand stilled in her hair. She felt the weight of his gaze upon her.

"I don't understand. Why?"

Sasha detangled herself from him and moved to lean against the island. Immediately she felt the loss of his heat. But she needed to think about this and she couldn't do that with him here, in her space.

"Because I need to think and ... and you are a distraction," she said honestly finally lifting her gaze to meet his.

Dylan moved to stand in front of her. He rubbed his hands up and down her arms, moving his body against hers. There was no denying how she affected him. The proof was displayed for all to see. And it excited her to know she was the cause of the bulge pressed suggestively against her.

"Yeah, the same could be said about you. Do you feel what you do to me?" He whispered in her ear as he lightly ran his tongue along the outside of her ear. "How about we distract each other?"

Sasha couldn't stop the chills running up and down her spine at the thought of what kind of distraction he had in mind. Her resolve began to waiver. Not wanting him to see the war being waged within herself, she lowered her gaze and put some space between them. She needed time to think this thing through and she couldn't do that with him here. She ran her fingers through her braids before lifting her gaze to his stormy blue eyes.

"No," she said on a breathy whisper.

"Dylan, I can no longer deny I have feelings for you and I'm pretty sure I'd like to explore them. But this is all new to me. I don't do casual sex and I've never gotten involved with a white man before. So I just need some time to make sure this is something I can handle."

A myriad of emotions passed across his face. Each one caused her heart to sink a little further. She didn't want him to think she was some kind of tease because nothing could be farther from the truth. Her insides were doing flips just standing this close to him and god help her but a part of her wanted him to convince her she didn't need to think just feel.

"Okay," he said leaning down to kiss her softly against her temple before moving away from her.

Shock caused her feet to remain rooted to her spot in the kitchen. Okay? Is that all he was going to say? Just okay? Sasha knew she should be relieved he had agreed to do it her way, but she couldn't deny she was a little disappointed that he was ... well doing it her way. She chanced a glance over at where he stood leaning against the doorframe looking down at the floor. This is what you wanted remember that, she told herself as she forced her legs to move. She slowly walked ahead of him to the front door trying to calm the raging war going on between her body and her brain. Would she ever know peace again? Sasha turned to find herself inches from Dylan's chest. She stepped back to allow some space, but he quickly crowded her against the front door, his hands on both sides of her head.

"We'll play this your way Sasha and I'll give you time to think because I want you to be okay with what's happening between us. I don't have all the answers but I know what I want. And I want you to want it too."

With that said he claimed her mouth again. Gone was the tentative kiss they'd shared moments ago. This was a more confident taking. One that showed her without a doubt what she was kicking out of her house tonight.

***

Dylan called himself all kinds of a fool as he drove away.

"Said she needed time to think. Why do women always want to think things to death?" he mumbled to the empty car.

It was a serious character flaw of the whole damn species in his opinion. But still he'd managed to walk away to give her the time she'd said she needed but it was with a cost. He had a raging hard on and it was damned uncomfortable to drive.

"Dammit," he cursed aloud.

Why hadn't he pushed the issue? She'd wanted him as much as he'd wanted her. He knew it. He'd felt the way her nipples had hardened at his touch. And the way she'd just kissed him. He would have thought it impossible for his dick to get any harder but it did at the thought of her moans and the way she had moved against him. His dick threatened to burst free of his pants. Dammit, he cursed again. He hated cold showers.

Dylan was about to exit onto the highway when his cell phone rang. He reached for it in the console between his seats.

"Hello," he answered gruffly.

"Come back now," Sasha's husky voice came through on the other end.

He slammed on breaks thankful there was nothing behind him and pulled out of the exit lane for the interstate.

"What? I thought you said you needed time to think about what you were doing," he said looking for a place to make a U-turn.

"I thought about it already. It took me a whole two minutes from the time you walked to your car and I closed my door, to realize what an idiot I am. I want you and that's all I need to know for now. The rest I'll figure it out later."

This was what he wanted. Had just been beating himself up over. And she'd come to this conclusion on her own. He hadn't he even had to push the issue. Yet he found himself hesitating. He didn't want her to have regrets in the morning. He wanted what they had to be the beginning of something. He could understand the want and the need. His body was screaming at him to turn the hell around while his brain was telling him to wait. When the hell did I get all these morals, he asked himself, knowing his desires would go unfulfilled tonight. He made a U-turn and headed back to the interstate and home.

"Look Sasha. I want what we have to be special the first time. I want it to be the beginning of something. Not just a night of sex."

Though what she offered held some definite appeal he knew it wasn't how he wanted it to be in the long run. He'd meant what he said about wanting this to be the beginning of something between them.

"So I'm gonna go on home, have a cold shower and a shot of something 80 proof."

"But I need you. I don't want to go to bed feeling like this? My whole body is on fire. It's aching for you," she said her voice husky with need and longing.

Dear god. Was this a test? He felt his body respond to the need in her voice and wondered if his zipper would hold. He briefly thought of trying to adjust himself but decided against that course of action. If he started he was scared he'd end up on the side of the road whacking off like some damn pervert.

"I know how you feel sweetheart. But you said it yourself. You're not used to doing anything like this. I can respect you for admitting you need time to think this thing through before just jumping in head first. I don't want there to be any regrets later."

He'd made the right decision.

"Now talk to me while I drive home," he said, having exited onto the interstate.

"I want you to stop being so damned rational and come back and fuck me. How's that for conversation," she said her voice coming out in a huff.

His dick responded instantly. This was going to be a long drive home.

Chapter 13

Sasha rolled over in bed the next morning feeling absolutely drained. She hadn't gotten to sleep until the sun was peeking through the blinds. She had talked to Dylan during his long drive home and then for some time after he'd gotten there. It had been almost four o'clock when they'd reluctantly gotten off the phone. She groaned as she recalled their conversation. Had she really begged him to come back and have sex with her last night? Where had all of her self control gone not to mention her dignity? Both seemed to be nonexistent when it came to Dylan. No man had ever made her feel so many emotions, each one more intense than the next.

Turning onto her side, she tucked her arm under the pillow. Her hand brushed against something hard. Sasha sat up in bed, pushing her loose braids out of her eyes, and looked under the pillow. She felt her face heat and her cunt spasm as her eyes lit upon the vibrator.

It had been a gift from Cat for her thirtieth birthday. When she'd seen it nestled in the folds of tissue paper, she'd wanted to sink through the floor in embarrassment. She had tucked the box at the back of her closet to make sure it would never be accidentally seen while looking for something else. And that was where it had sat unused until the wee hours of this morning when her body had demanded fulfillment and her own fingers were neither long enough nor thick enough to give the much needed relief she'd craved.

    Sasha leaned back against the pillows and examined the thick head of the vibrator, running the tip of her finger over the rounded head and down the thickly ribbed shaft. She felt her body quiver as she recalled how those ridges had felt rubbing along the sensitive insides of her tender cunt. When she'd finally shoved it deep inside her hot and wet tunnel she'd gasped as the breath had left her body at the pleasure of having something so thick inside her. Over and over again she'd shoved it into her quivering flesh always a fraction of an inch away from that all too elusive spot she needed to reach to obtain maximum pleasure. Finally frustrated with not being able to cum she'd remembered Cat's recommended positions. Sasha could laugh now over how she'd almost fallen off her tall bed trying to reach the discarded packaging on the floor and keep the vibrator deeply inserted in her cunt. She'd read the different positions as she'd slowly moved the massive object in and out of her to keep her senses on edge. When her eyes spotted bold lettering she'd felt moisture leak from her center and roll down between her ass cheeks. Before she could give it too much thought she'd pulled the vibrator from her wet lips and moved to her knees her legs spread wide. She'd raised herself up a little and placed the base of the vibrator down on the bed. The head, now glistening with her moisture, pointed straight up as if it were waiting for her. Rising up a little higher on her knees she moved over the waiting head and sank down. She'd not been able to restrain the groan of pleasure she'd felt over having her cunt stretched once again to its full capacity. It'd taken her a few attempts to find her rhythm with no one under her to hold her upright but once she'd found the motion she needed to obtain complete pleasure she'd allowed her thoughts to run free.

With one hand holding the base in place her other had been free to caress her small breasts. The already hardened nipples had been pinched and pulled. With each tug on the pebble hard nubs she'd felt a quiver in her stomach. The vibrator had disappeared to be replaced by Dylan's hard, thick length thrusting up into her waiting and hot cavern. Her juices had rolled down along the sides of his hard shaft each time she'd pulled up and with each decent she'd heard the squish and her juices had flowed even more. As she'd ridden him for all she was worth she picked up the pace and began dropping all her weight back down allowing the head to finally graze that elusive spot. A groan escaped her open mouth as her orgasm lingered just outside her reach. Strong fingers moved from her nipples slowly down her taut stomach to between her legs. They played briefly in her low cut bush, grazing her swollen clit on purpose before moving away to caress her tensed ass cheeks. But as if they could not resist the hand returned to her throbbing bud moving with more force against her clit. Sure fingers rubbed it into a swollen hard point to match the nipples they'd been playing with a few moments ago. She'd felt the orgasm building deep inside her and as she'd plunged down one final time she'd screamed her pleasure as she finally hit that spot full on and her cunt began to pulse and juices began to gush from her. Her body pulled up once more. She felt the multiple ridges massaging the sides of sensitive flesh and she dropped all her weight down and felt her orgasm take complete control of her as her cunt muscles spasmed around the thick dick buried so deep inside of her. She immediately felt another orgasm take control after the first one faded as her inner muscles continued to massage the hardened length inside of her.

Sasha fell forward on the bed, her face buried in the pillow, as she tried to control her breathing after such a powerful orgasm. Her memories of last night and what had just happened became intertwined. She shifted to bring her arms from beneath the weight of her body and felt her cunt spasm again around the vibrator still inserted deep inside her walls. Oh god. She'd had the damn thing for three years and had never used it once and now she'd used it twice within hours of each other.

Rolling to her back Sasha reached between her legs and pulled the vibrator slowly from her swollen cunt. She should have been prepared for the way it felt moving from her channel but she still gasped at the pleasure of it and had to fight the urge to shove it back inside. She pushed the covers aside and got up from bed. Her legs were weak from their kneeling position on the bed causing her to move cautiously across her large bedroom towards her master bath taking the vibrator with her. She cleaned it and put it back in the box, returning it to its original place at the back of her closet. A small smile tilted her lips up as she hoped she'd never have to resort to using it again.

During the night she had come to grips with a few things. Her want of Dylan being one of them and the other being the fact she wanted to see where things could go between them if given a chance. She realized this meant going against every rule she had but she felt as if she'd be cheating herself if she didn't.

"I need a hot shower and some coffee," she mumbled to herself.

Knowing she would be in the shower awhile, Sasha decided to put the coffee on first. She briefly contemplated putting on her robe to cover the short t-shirt she'd worn to bed the night before but disregarded it as a waste of time. She was heading back upstairs by way of the back steps off of her laundry room when her doorbell rang. She glanced at the clock over the stove. It was barely eight o'clock. It wasn't unusual for her friends to come over for coffee or an early session at the gym, but not knowing how her evening with Dylan might end she'd thought she'd canceled any plans. Oh well, if she hadn't it would do her good to go to the gym. Maybe work off a little frustration.

Sasha opened her door, hiding herself behind it as best she could, all too aware of how little she had on. But when she saw Dylan standing there she stepped from behind the door and opened it a little wider. Her body's response to seeing the man she'd longed to have lying between her legs last night and this morning was immediate and intense.

"May I come in?" he asked his hands shoved down in the front pockets of his jeans.

His look was a little hesitant as he stood there. She didn't think she had ever seen him in jeans before. Her hungry gaze roamed over him. Everything this man put on made him look hot. Stepping back, she allowed him to enter. She leaned against the coolness of her front door hoping it would help reduce her body's temperature which had been rising slowly since she'd opened the door. She realized she probably should have felt some kind of embarrassment over her state of undress but she quickly pushed the thought to the back of her mind. Before this day was over she planned to be in his presence with even less clothes on.

"This is a pleasant surprise," she said, her fingers itching to reach out and smooth the material of his t-shirt over his chest.

Patience she told herself. You'll get the opportunity to touch every inch of him in time.

"I hope you don't mind my not calling first," he asked and Sasha could hear the uncertainty in his voice.

"No that's fine. Would you like some coffee? I just put some on. It should be ready now," she said and moved towards the kitchen without waiting for his reply.

She felt his eyes upon her as she moved about the kitchen getting cups out of the cabinet. The hem of her t-shirt moved up to graze against the curve of her butt as she stood on tip toes to reach them. Sasha glanced back over her shoulder to find his heated gaze staring back at her. Her hands trembled as she carefully carried the cups over to the coffee pot.

"Would you like cream, sugar?"

Or me, she added in her head. She barely stifled the giggle bubbling up at the inane thought. She filled two cups and moved back towards the island where she carefully placed both cups on the marble surface.

"No black is fine thanks," he replied shifting a little on the barstool.

She filed that bit of information away for later use and headed towards the refrigerator to get out creamer for her coffee. Her departure was halted when she felt a gentle tug on her hand.

"Sasha."

The voice that called her name was thick and strained with an emotion she couldn't define. Dylan pulled her back to stand between his open legs. Trembling hands brought her chin up to meet his stormy gaze.

"Please forgive me for not being strong enough to honor your wishes," he said before lowering his mouth to hers.

She didn't get the chance to tell him it was okay before his soft lips took hers in a kiss so gentle it threatened to bring her to tears. His hand gripped the back of her head and quickly tangled his fingers in her hair. He held her steady as he inserted his tongue between her parted lips and proceeded to plunder her mouth. A gasp of shock escaped her when his tongue began massaging the tender insides of her top and bottom lips. Pleasure ran through her body. His hands moved down to pull her hips closer to the center of his heat. A rush of moisture flooded her already drenched panties. Oh God she needed him closer. She twined her arms around his waist and closed the distance remaining between them. Oh yes that was much better, she thought as she rubbed herself against his swollen hardness. She pulled his shirt from where it was tucked into the waistband of his jeans. She needed to feel his skin. Wanted to kiss every inch of it.

 Finally after what seemed like hours and mere moments at the same time, Dylan lifted his head to allow them a breath. But his lips weren't idle. Sasha moved her head to the side as they kissed their way across her jaw down the slender line of her neck. The tender kisses he placed along his route caused shivers to run through her body.

 "I need you Sasha," he moaned against her shoulder.

 Her head fell back as his hands traveled down the backs of her thighs back up to cup her ass. When his hands moved inside her panties to cup her naked flesh her knees buckled. She reached for Dylan's shoulders for support. Determined fingers pulled her cheeks apart and ran a finger along the crease. He played around the rim of her puckered hole before moving lower to place a long finger at the center of her moisture, causing Sasha to gasp in pleasure. Another finger joined in. They moved in and out, stretching her at the odd angle. Her body greedily accepted them but she needed more. Her mouth opened to tell him but no words came out. She couldn't think beyond what he was doing to her. His hot mouth nibbling at her shoulder. His fingers thrusting deeper inside of her. She stood on tiptoes, which brought her nipples in contact with his open mouth. Apparently understanding her request, Dylan quickly caught the cotton covered nub in his mouth. The pleasure of his fingers inserted deep inside and her nipple in the hot cavern of his mouth was too much for her. Sasha moved against the fingers thrusting in and out of her pussy searching for release.

"Please Dylan. I need to cum," she begged.

"You will baby trust me," he said releasing her nipple. He moved down to take her mouth plunging his tongue deep inside as his fingers moved for deeper access between her legs.

The familiar pressure of a powerful orgasm pulled at her as she rode the fingers plundering her dripping pussy.

She felt him pull them free of her clenching lips to move them around the outside of her anus. She'd never had anyone play with that part of her body before and felt excitement run through her. Fear of pain and possible pleasure making her body react even more. She jerked at the first push of his finger into her puckered hole. Her stomach muscles tensed.

"Relax sweetheart," he whispered against her swollen mouth before bending his head to once again capture a nipple through the thin material of her t-shirt.

She gasped at the pull of his mouth on her breast and barely felt his further intrusion into her ass. When he began moving smoothly in an out with one finger she relaxed against him, her head on his chest. She concentrated on forcing air in and out of her lungs. A matching finger plunging into her pussy soon joined the twisting finger in her ass. The two together drove her over the edge she had been trying to reach since his first touch. She clenched her teeth to keep the scream from escaping her parted lips as her orgasm washed over her. Her head felt heavy as she came down from her incredible high. Her body was still pulsing. She wanted more. Much more.

"See I told you I'd let you cum," Dylan said as he pulled his now drenched fingers from between her legs and lightly caressed her ass and thighs.

"Hmm," she said not able to quite form words yet.

With a struggle she lifted her head and caught her breath at the emotions reflected in his eyes. She lifted a trembling hand to caress the side of his strong jaw and felt a tug at her heart. She stepped out of his arms and reached for his hand. Sasha paused briefly at the foot of her stairs. Last minute doubts over her actions causing her hesitation. Taking him to her bedroom would forever imprint memories of him there. Did she want to do that? What if things didn't work out? She'd always considered her bedroom her own private haven.

"We don't have to do this if you're not ready," he said massaging her now tense shoulders.

Hearing him offer her a way out knowing how much he wanted it made up her mind. She couldn't imagine any other man except the one at her back offering to walk away with no release for themselves. Certainly no man she'd met before. The action endeared him to her even more and she didn't think he had any idea. She glanced at him over her shoulder and threw him what she hoped was a seductive smile.

"You're not getting out of it this time. So I hope you checked your morals at the door," she said pulling him up the steps.

Changing the Rules

"I guess it's a good thing then that I left them and all shame at home this morning when I came to beg you to put me out my misery," came the deep reply from close behind her.

The pause at what she considered her secret door was only long enough to allow time to try and calm down her runaway nerves. No man had ever entered this room. As she stepped to the side and allowed Dylan to enter she couldn't take her eyes off of him as he took in her private haven.

When she'd bought the house she'd done so at the beginning of construction and had a hand in the design of the rooms somewhat. She'd deliberately bought a four-bedroom home so she could have her own private sanctuary increased. The room they'd entered through was her sitting room and office area. This room was separated from her bedroom by a set of French doors that were open allowing for a clear view of her massive bed. It had been an indulgence that her friends to this day kidded her for. Such a petite woman with a California King was almost laughable. Glancing back at the large frame of the man standing quietly behind her, she realized she may have the last laugh after all.

Sasha led the way through the sitting area into her bedroom having seen the spark of interest in Dylan's eyes as he gazed through the open doors. She watched as he took in his new surroundings. When she'd decorated she'd used a lot of rich reds and golds, trying to create a desert getaway for herself. She'd done so strictly for her own pleasure. The sheer gold material flowing down from the supports of her four-poster bed had been whimsy on her part. She hoped he didn't see it as too childish.

"You have a beautiful bedroom," he said walking over to the bed. His fingers lightly ran across her sheets. "These are much softer than mine."

"High thread count," she replied absently, feeling shy all of a sudden.

The heat from downstairs though not completely gone, had cooled somewhat as she waited for his opinion of her private domain. She became aware of his gaze focused on her and a shiver moved through her.

"Come here Sasha," he beckoned from where he stood beside her bed.

She walked slowly towards him and into his open arms. The breath she'd been holding since they had entered her bedroom was released as she savored the feel of his arms around her slender frame. It felt so good just to have him hold her, but her body quickly reminded her it wanted more. Sasha stepped out of his embrace and pushed him backwards closer to her bed. Memories of her earlier actions had her wondering if she should change her sheets. Dylan's grip on her hips pulling her against him chased the thought from her mind. What difference did it make anyway they'd just get them dirty again. Besides she felt kind of naughty knowing what she'd done earlier and was about to do now. They'd just become her favorite sheets.

"I have wanted you since the moment I saw you rushing across that damn lobby," Dylan said as he ran his hands over her body.

"I wanted the same thing only I just didn't want to admit it."

Her head fell back and her eyes closed against the pleasure of his touch. His hands slid down the back of her panties and pulled her neatly into the nook between his legs. His long fingers inserted themselves once again between the cheeks of her ass and began running lightly along her crease.

"And now?" he asked his hot breath against her ear.

A gasp escaped her open lips at the feel of his finger thrusting deep into her ready pussy.

"Now," she panted unable to gather her senses. "Now I want it even more."

Lifting up on her toes, she took his mouth in a soul consuming kiss. She pushed her tongue into his open mouth and began to taste him. It made her head spin. She moved restlessly against him, rubbing her heated center against his hardened length. Strong fingers tightened against her hips holding them in place. She watched as he took a steadying breath.

"Sasha I only have the strength to offer you one final out. I don't think, no I know, I don't have the strength or willpower to stop once we begin." Dylan stared deep into her brown eyes.

A soft smile came to her face as she gazed at the man who had caused so many changes to occur in such a short period of time. She just knew it would take a lifetime to figure him out as well as the power he seemed to have over her. It should have frightened her to think how badly she wanted to take the time to find out.

"Thanks for the offer but I'm tired of denying myself what I want. And what I want Mr. Matthews is for you to stop talking and make love to me."

No sooner were the words out of her mouth than Dylan lifted her from her feet and placed her on the bed. He quickly moved on top of her, nestling between her spread legs. It brought his hardened dick in direct contact with her throbbing clit. Strong fingers buried deep into her hair and his mouth lowered to devour hers with all the passion he'd been holding back. Sasha met him with a passion of her own, leaving them both panting for breath as he lifted his mouth from her swollen lips. He ran his fingers beneath her t-shirt, which had ridden up her thighs, to cup her naked breasts, pinching and pulling on her sensitive nubs. She tried to move beneath him but his weight kept her still.

"Dylan please," she panted.

"Please what?" he asked pushing her t-shirt up and over her head, his gaze locked on her breasts.

"You have beautiful breasts," he said before lowering his head to take her nipples in his mouth.

Pleasure spiraled through her and stopped between her thighs. Each tug on her nipple brought a new throbbing from her swollen clit.

"Dylan I need..." Sasha moaned desire running through her.

He leaned close to her ear, taking her lobe in his hot mouth.

"You need what sweetheart? Tell me."

The words refused to form. She had never been this on fire for a man in her life. Maybe she could show him. She struggled to make room between them for her trembling hands to undo the buttons of his jeans. One slender hand reached inside his boxers to caress the soft hardness that was Dylan. Her thumb rubbed along the thick vein on the underside of his dick. A tortured groan from the man above her sounded next to her ear where he'd laid his head the moment she'd touched him.

"Let me help you out sweetheart," he said getting off of her suddenly to remove his clothes. "There that's better," he said standing proudly beside the bed in all his nakedness.

Her breath caught in her chest as she took in the sight of him. He was gorgeous. There was a light scattering of dark hairs from his chest down his flat stomach. His dick stood out in front of him in all its glory, the head slightly red and swollen. Her tongue darted out to lick dry lips. She'd never been one for oral sex but just staring at Dylan's straining member had her craving to take him in her mouth. She reached a hand tentatively out to touch him. She ran her hand from the base of his dick to the head and squeezed. The contrast in how soft he was yet hard at the same time was mind boggling. Her past sexual experiences, the few there had been, had not prepared her for this. Of that she was certain. She felt it to her bones that she was about to have her world rocked on so many levels.

Dylan ran his hands along the tops of her thighs to her waist. He tugged at the waistband of her panties and she lifted her hips so he could remove them. The heat in his gaze as he roamed over her naked body almost brought on her orgasm. It turned her on to no end. His look spoke of how much he wanted her.

"You are beautiful," he whispered hoarsely, his gaze still roving over her.

"So are you," she whispered back, her eyes still glued to his still growing hardness in her hand.

A deep chuckle came from Dylan causing her to raise her glazed over brown eyes. He moved on top of her once more when she opened her arms for him to come to her. Sasha wrapped her slender arms around him and held him tight. She'd waited so long for this moment. If felt like longer than the few weeks they had known each other. It felt like it had taken a lifetime for her to get to this moment. She had thought to savor the moment but her body was on fire and her need for Dylan burned deep in her veins.

"Dylan please make love to me," she whispered against his ear.

Without warning she found herself staring down into his desire filled blue eyes. Her knees automatically went to each side of his hips. His large dick nestled itself between her legs. Pre-cum leaked from the swollen head. She reached her hand down and stroked.

"Would you like to help me with this," Dylan asked handing her a condom.

Her face flamed with embarrassment. She hadn't thought about protection at all. Just getting him inside her so she could relieve the constant ache she felt. With trembling fingers she reached for the condom. She was all too aware of his heated gaze watching her every move. Once finished, she looked up and was shocked to see the pained expression on his face.

"That's what you call sweet torture," he said as he pulled her down for his kiss.

Pulling away, she raised herself up and moved over the straining head of his dick. A gasp left her parted lips as she sank down. Pausing halfway, she stopped to catch her breath. A hand on Dylan's chest helped hold herself up. Her body demanded she plunge down and fill it completely but luckily common sense prevailed. She realized she needed time to adjust to his size.

"Are you alright," he asked.

Sasha heard the strain in his voice. Probably from his efforts to remain perfectly still. She managed to give him a small smile.

"I just need a minute. It's been awhile and I've never taken anyone as large as you before."

Taking a deep breath, she rose up slightly before continuing her slow decent once more. The lips of her cunt stretched further around his massive width. Up and down she continued slowly until she finally had him all inside of her. She raised her head to gaze at him, a triumphant smile on her face. But he didn't see. His eyes were closed and she noticed his jaw was clenched tight. She leaned down and softly placed a kiss on his closed mouth. She was ready to give them both what they wanted. Slowly at first she moved to find her rhythm. She wasn't able to contain the groan of pleasure that left her lips with each downward motion. Feeling more comfortable and unable to hold back any longer, her speed increased. Dylan's lids opened to reveal lust filled eyes.

"Dylan I need you to move," she managed to gasp.

He gripped her hips tightly before his hard, thick length thrust up into her waiting and hot cavern. Over and over he thrust into her heated center. Faster and faster. Her juices rolled down along the sides of his hard dick. She quickly picked up on the rhythm of his movements and each time he pulled out she rose up. She began dropping all her weight back down each time he thrust within her allowing the head to finally graze that elusive spot.

"Oh god Sasha. I don't know how much longer I can hold off. I'm so close," Dylan groaned.

A groan escaped her open mouth as her orgasm lingered just outside her reach. One of Dylan's hands moved from her hips across her taut stomach to between her legs. They played briefly in her low cut bush, grazing her swollen clit on purpose before moving away to grip her tensed ass cheeks. But as if they could not resist the hand returned to her throbbing bud moving with more force against her clit.

"Oh Dylan," Sasha moaned.

She felt the orgasm building deep inside her. She plunged down one final time and screamed her pleasure. Sasha's cunt began to pulse and juices began to gush from her.

She heard Dylan's answering shout of pleasure as he continued to thrust up into her sending her body into another shudder. She dropped all her weight down and felt her orgasm take complete control of her as her cunt muscles spasmed around the thick dick buried so deep inside of her.

Chapter 14

Sasha woke to the gentle caress of Dylan's hand running up and down the outside of her leg, which was thrown across his thigh. For a few moments she just lay there and allowed memories of how they'd spent the day to take her back. The smile she felt lifting her swollen lips gave way to a giggle. If her friends only knew "that thinks too much" and "always in control" Sasha had just had wild uninhibited sex. Oh god they'd die. She covered her mouth as another giggle escaped her lips.

"Hey, what's so funny? This is supposed to be a time to reflect on the wonders of my lovemaking," Dylan said rising on an elbow with his open palm supporting his head to stare down at her.

She put her hand more securely over her mouth but the thought of the surprised faces of her friends caused another giggle to escape.

"So are you gonna share the joke?"

She reached for his face and pulled it down close to hers and kissed him. She could still taste her juices on the tongue he thrust into her mouth. With a sense of surprise that she could still want him just as much as before her first taste of him, she felt her juices begin to flow. Now familiar with his body, she reached between them, grabbed his hardening cock and began stroking it.

"I was simply thinking of what my friends would say if they knew I had spent the morning, afternoon and...," Sasha glanced at the clock on her bedside table. Five o'clock.

"And the early part of the evening making love to the sexiest man I've ever met."

Dylan's breath came out in short gasps as she continued to stroke his dick. She gripped him a little tighter and continued moving her hand along the length of him from base to tip before venturing down his shaft to caress his balls. He fell back on the bed as the air rushed from his lungs. During their marathon of love making she'd learned how to get him excited and she used all of what she'd learned now. Sasha moved to her knees. Her legs spread seductively giving him a view of her exposed pussy, which was glistening with new moisture. Her head bowed over the prize, her mouth slightly open, she slowly licked her lips. Dylan gave a small whimper as he waited for her to lower her head and take him into the warm cavern of her mouth. When Sasha finally lowered her head she heard a groan of pleasure from him. The sound filled her with unimagined power as well as proceeded to turn her on even more. She licked the sides of his dick with her tongue while she continued to keep him a prisoner of her mouth. When she lifted so just the swollen head was in her mouth she licked with quick strokes. Tiny shivers moved through his body.

"Dear god Sasha," Dylan moaned aloud.

He gripped the sheets with white knuckles when the tip of his dick met the back of her throat. The groan that escaped his lips was one of pleasure and torture. His mouth slightly open, he leaned up to see her working more of his now glistening dick into her willing mouth before he fell backwards onto the bed once more. His head thrashed back and forth on the pillow as he tried to fight the urge to thrust his hips. It became harder when Sasha's hand came up to capture his balls.

"Oh sweetheart that's it take it all into your hot mouth," he groaned.

Her naked ass bounced up and down in the air in time with her strokes on his dick. Dylan reached over and palmed the ass that was just inches from his face. He inserted two fingers deep into her dripping pussy and twisted so his knuckles grazed the inside of her tender flesh.

Sasha's head came up and she gasped at the feeling of his stretching her.

"Oh... oh that feels so good," she breathed.

"So does what you're doing. Don't stop. I wanna cum in your mouth," he said grabbing the leg closest to him.

He pulled it over his head, giving him full access to her wide open pussy. As she moved to take him once again into her hot mouth, Dylan was poised to get a taste of the clit poking out through her dark bush. At the first touch of her tongue on his dick, he pulled her hips down to meet his face and opened his mouth wide over her opening.

"Oh god," Sasha shrieked in surprise, coming up off of his dick with a pop.

"Don't stop. I want us to cum together and I'm already half way there," he said against her swollen clit.

She picked up the pace as she took him deeper into her mouth. She began using her hand to stroke up and down along with her mouth. Each time she descended she took him deeper.

Dylan licked the dripping pussy in his face from her puckered asshole to her open and ready hole. He flattened his tongue and pushed it into her opening and he felt a pause on his dick.

Changing the Rules

"You like that don't you sweetheart," he asked his words vibrating against her tender lips.

He pushed two fingers deep into her and another finger he inserted it into her asshole. He began slowly moving all three fingers in and out of their respective holes as Sasha continued her steady stroke on his dick. Wanting to cum at the same time when her stroke on his dick increased so did his thrusts into her dripping holes. Dylan's balls tightened painfully against his body in preparation for his orgasm and Sasha's muscles tightened around his fingers.

Sasha lifted all the way off of Dylan's dick and took him deep within the confines of her hot mouth in one downward stroke. He easily slid across her flattened tongue. His balls drew closer to his body and his dick hardened painfully as his cum shot its way up and out of the swollen head of his dick, which was now buried down her throat. He could feel her swallowing and it massaged the entire length of his dick.

Dylan renewed the stroke of his fingers in and out of her pussy and ass, taking her clit between his lips and sucking hard. He felt her body jerk but he continued sucking until he felt the first gush of her juices flow across his fingers. He removed his hands and placed his mouth over her open hole pushing his tongue into the opening to gather all of her juices as they flowed down. He sucked again on her clit and a fresh wave of liquid flooded his mouth. He drank like a starving man. One final swipe of his tongue made sure he'd captured all of her juices before he fell back on the bed exhausted. His dick popped free of her mouth and she moved to lay beside him with a deep sigh.

"I don't think I can move," she said her eyes closed.

Dylan laughed beside her, "I know the feeling."

He turned on his side and gathered her in his arms. He reached to pull the covers over their naked spent bodies. Sasha turned to face him in his arms, feeling more safe and secure than she'd ever felt. This was where she wanted to stay. But concerns she'd managed to push away all day came back. Nothing could change the dynamics of their professional relationship. Technically he was her boss plus he'd been the one to hire her. If their relationship came into the light there would be speculation running rampant she was certain of it. Sure she and Dylan would know the truth but she didn't want anything to tarnish the reputation she was working hard to establish. And then there was the fact Dylan moved in a different world than she did. A deep sigh left her. How could she have failed to recognize him when she'd first seen him in the elevator? His face was always paired with some other equally gorgeous female. White female, she felt the need to add. She still felt a little guilty about the research she'd done on him after their first encounter. But she'd needed to know what she was dealing with and research was what she did for a living. She'd seen enough to know she didn't want that life.

When she'd pulled up the newspaper archives for the society section, it had amazed her how many pictures there were of him. Photos taken of him going into expensive restaurants downtown. Dylan at the opera. Several pictures of him at the governor of Illinois' fundraiser a few months back. Man did he have a thing for blondes. Tall blondes. She almost laughed at the thought. For more months than she cared to recall it seemed his face had been everywhere and then all of a sudden nothing. Being the researcher she was, she had double checked and hadn't found one picture in six months. Even though she'd been still adamantly denying any feelings for Dylan one way or the other, there was no denying not seeing any pictures of him had brought on a feeling of relief. Even he had to get tired of it eventually. Right?

Dylan's arms tightened around her and pulled her closer to the heat of his body.

"Stop thinking so hard. I can hear it all the way over here and I'm trying to take a nap," he said sleep heavy in his voice.

"I can't help it."

One lid lifted to stare down at her.

"You're not regretting today are you?"

"No never. I loved every minute of it," she said reaching up to smooth the frown that had appeared between his eyebrows.

He leaned down and kissed the tip of her nose.

"Good. So get some rest for now and whatever it is we'll deal with it later."

Sasha closed her eyes and breathed in the deep the scent of their love making but her thoughts continued their efforts to beat her down. She snuggled even closer allowing him to fill her senses in hopes it would occupy her over active mind. Maybe she was just over thinking the situation. It wouldn't be the first time it'd happened. If their relationship continued to grow and became common knowledge a few people might voice concerns about how she'd gotten her job. But by then Sasha hoped she'd had enough time to prove to Michael and her fellow co-workers she deserved to be there. At least she felt better about Dylan's popularity with the press. It appeared he'd run his course and they had moved on to someone else. At least she sure hoped so because she was a simple person and didn't want her love life spread all over the pages of the paper for everyone to read about and judge.

Chapter 15

Sasha sat on one of the four bar stools at the granite tiled island in Dylan's oversized kitchen and watched him move comfortably around the large space. He was marinating steaks they'd picked up on the way to his house. Since they'd spent all day Saturday at her place, he'd decided it was his turn to play host for Sunday. So they'd gotten up early this morning and taken a long shower. One that had resulted in their having to take another one, she recalled laughing.

"Are you sure I can't help you with the steaks or anything else?"

She felt slightly guilty about sitting there doing nothing while he did the bulk of the work for their afternoon meal. She had already finished fixing their salad and it was in the frig chilling.

Dylan turned to look at her over his shoulder with a devilish smile on his face.

"Positive. I had planned to fix steaks this weekend so I had already chopped onions, peppers and fresh mushrooms. They're in the refrigerator, waiting to be put on the grill. So you just sit there looking gorgeous and let me do this. I'm almost done," he said winking at her.

Her heart skipped a beat. He had been giving her compliments all day and each one had made her heart turn over. Not to mention her body was on a slow burn from the intensity in his gaze when he looked at her. Sasha would have thought after having spent all day yesterday in bed she'd have better control over her hormones. But if anything the opposite were true. She found something erotic in everything he did. Her gaze fell to where he stood working with the steaks. He was massaging seasonings into the meat. The look on his face led her to believe he might be thinking of something other than the steak beneath his fingers. The more she watched those fingers the hotter she got. She tore her gaze reluctantly away and tried to get control of her breathing. She glanced up at him to see if he'd noticed the changes. There was a small smile on his face which led her to believe he knew exactly what he was doing to her. She wished she could be angry. Instead she found herself growing hungrier for something other than food. She was sure it wouldn't take much to change his mind about eating steak and interest him in eating her instead. Her thoughts surprised her. When had she become so wanton? Just the thought brought a smile to her face. Her, Sasha Jordan, a closet wanton woman.

"Will we be eating in the dining room?" She asked trying to bring her mind out of the gutter where it was currently residing.

Dylan, having finished his task, washed his hands and wiped them on a dishtowel. He put the aluminum foil wrapped steaks on a tray he would be taking to the grill.

"In case you hadn't noticed, it's rather large. I want to be in the same zip code as you when we eat in case I get the urge to nibble on something else after we're done with the steaks," he said laughing, reaching over to give her a light kiss on her upturned lips.

The kiss was over too soon for Sasha's liking.

"It is huge. Why do you have it if you don't really use it?"

Dylan hunched his shoulders, reached for his bottle of beer on the counter and took the seat across from her.

"I did a lot of renovations on the house before I moved in. When the house was near completion, the decorator saw the size of the dining area and said it just had to have a certain kind of table. One that made a statement. I only use it when I have the occasional sit down dinner party. For most of my meals, I take them upstairs in my office. When the weather's nice, I eat on the balcony or the deck. But for our purposes, since this is a barbeque of sorts, we will be eating on the deck. If that's okay with you?"

"You have a balcony?"

Dylan laughed at the look on her face and motioned for her to follow him out of the kitchen. She didn't recall seeing a balcony when they had driven up. She felt sure she would have noticed one during her first look at the place he called home. She had known to expect wealth but she hadn't been prepared for the size of his home on the outside or the inside when she had walked through the foyer.

She followed him as he led the way upstairs to what he considered his private domain. Even before Dylan had confirmed it, Sasha had figured a professional had done the lower levels, just as she could tell as she moved up the spiral staircase he had done the upper levels. While the lower level was meant to be a showcase of his wealth and standing in the Chicago society, the upper level was meant to make a statement about the man. Who he was and what he was about. Sasha found she preferred the upper level.

She followed him down a long hall, passing a few rooms that didn't have any furniture. She figured they were extra bedrooms waiting to be done. But then she passed a room that could only be his office. She paused before the door and felt drawn inside. Now this was Dylan.

Changing the Rules

The room had a magnificent view of the backyard with ceiling to floor windows to the left and behind the mahogany desk that commanded the majority of the room. There was a massive bookshelf built into the wall on the right. As Sasha stepped closer to examine it, she saw it held awards and certificates for community service and his charitable work, along with pictures of Dylan with the governor and senator of Illinois. The uneasy feeling from yesterday came back.

As she continued to move around the room, her gaze was drawn to the massive desk. It was positively huge. It held a laptop, printer and fax machine and still left a whole section bare. She walked over to touch the smooth surface of the desk. It was cool to the touch. She wondered how it would feel under her bare behind as Dylan laid her down on top of it to feast upon her body. She laughed at the thought. Was this really her thinking such naughty thoughts?

She felt his presence in the room before he even touched her. Strong arms encircled her waist, pulling her back against his hard chest. She felt his dick swell against her lower back and her body responded in turn. Sasha turned slowly, raising her arms to encircle his neck before pulling his head down to meet hers. Running her fingers through the hair at the nape of his neck, she began to explore his mouth with her tongue. She heard and felt his moan deep in his throat right before he lifted his mouth from hers, allowing them a much needed breath of air. She saw desire reflected in the blue gaze staring back at her but there was also something else lying in their depths. A shiver ran through her body at its intensity.

Unable to handle the brilliance of it any longer, she lowered her head and tried to pull out of his embrace, but Dylan held her fast. He reached down and lifted her chin so her gaze met his once again. Sasha had caught a glimpse of the intense emotion last night and this morning when she'd caught him looking at her before he'd turn away or hidden it. But it was at the front now for all to see.

"Don't run from it Sasha. I can't deny how I feel any longer. Nor do I want to. I want you in my life but I'm willing to give you time to decide if it's where you'd like to be too." Dylan tucked her against his chest and held her close.

Sasha closed her eyes and enjoyed just being held by this man. She realized this was what had been missing from her other relationships. With Dylan she felt as if she belonged to someone and he wasn't afraid to show her that with her was where he wanted to be. From the beginning he had never hidden the fact. Even during her two year relationship and engagement with Melvin she hadn't felt this connected to him. And she wanted this. She wanted to feel as if she belonged to someone. More specifically to belong to this man. The one who could make her insides turn over with just a look or one of his crooked grins. The man who made her want to forget all her rules and just live life, taking each day as it came. Being held within Dylan's embrace made all her doubts about their blossoming relationship seem unimportant and minute. It made her not care who knew they were together or who saw them. Let them talk.

***

Dylan could practically hear Sasha's mind working overtime. It had been like that every minute they hadn't been making love last night. It was one of the reasons he'd kept her busy thinking of other things until well into this morning. He smiled. Well that and the fact he couldn't seem to get enough of her. He'd taken great pleasure in exploring all the places they were different in coloring when she'd brought up their race difference again. He'd enjoyed himself even more exploring all the places on her body that were different shades of color. Then this morning on the drive to his house she had mentioned she didn't want her co-workers to think she'd earned her position by sleeping with him. He'd assured her that wouldn't happen and reminded her she was already earning a reputation for being dependable and capable of handling tough situations. She was making her own mark with the company and didn't need him to do that for her. He should be tired from all the potential pitfalls and hurdles he'd overcome. But at the root of all of them appeared to be the biggest issue yet – one Dylan hadn't even considered.

In some respects he lived a high profile life. His position as CFO of Presco put him in the limelight a lot and it also meant he brushed elbows with some of Chicago's wealthiest and most influential people. He'd never really given it much thought before Sasha had mentioned it but he guessed it could be a bit intimidating. All the other women he'd dated had counted this as a definite benefit to being with him. It put them right where they wanted to be and Dylan had never held any delusions about what they wanted from him. But Sasha was different. She didn't want any unnecessary attention turned her way. He found it slightly ironic how their biggest obstacle turned out to be his success when it was his success and position with Presco that had brought them together. Dylan was sure somewhere the fates were having a good laugh at his expense.

Never the less he would do whatever it took to keep this woman right were she was. It wasn't that big of a hardship for him to avoid the spotlight. He'd done it quite successfully over the last few months and had enjoyed not worrying about having cameras going off in his face or his picture plastered all over the papers. He definitely didn't miss the speculation about who he was dating and what it all meant if anything.

Sasha snuggled closer to him, rubbing her body against him restlessly. Dylan pulled back a little to gaze down into her brown eyes. His body trembled at what he saw. What started out as a gentle taking of her upturned lips turned quickly to a kiss full of heat and passion. He ran his fingers through her loose braids. And when she gasped he took full advantage of her open mouth and swooped in with his tongue.

Her hands ran up and down his broad back, what she could reach of it, before bringing them around between their bodies to caress his chest. Excitement raced through him at her touch. There was always such wonder on her face when she explored his body. It made him glad he'd been so vigilant about the gym. She unbuttoned his oxford shirt and pushed it back off his shoulders, he helped shrug it off the rest of the way. Her fingers danced over his heated skin until they centered on his hardened nipples. She licked a path from his breastbone to the tight little nubs where she pulled them into the warm cavern of her mouth. Dylan moaned his pleasure and pulled her closer to her target. She moved from one to the other and back again before moving further down his taut tanned stomach.

Sure hands rested at the waistband of his jeans before reaching for the buttons. He had to wonder were the timid shy woman from yesterday had gone. A part of him missed her but in her place was someone sure of her power over the man standing in front of her and her affect on his body. She knew where to touch to get the most intense reaction out of him. When he felt his jeans fall around his legs he looked down at the woman kneeling in front of him. Hair falling around her face, she impatiently pushed it back out of her way. Having pity, he reached down and pulled it back for her. She smiled up at him before turning her attention to the steepled front of his boxers. All thought left him as Sasha engulfed the boxer covered head of his dick, her mouth instantly soaking the front of his shorts. He rolled his head back on his neck and gave himself over to the feelings coursing through his body. He pulled her head closer as she began to move down his length to stroke his balls through his shorts.

"Oh god. That mouth of yours should be on a most dangerous list somewhere," he said on a groan as she pushed up one leg of his shorts to suck on his sac.

"Sasha..."

Changing the Rules

"Yes?" she asked looking up at him with an innocent look that belied the she-devil lying within her.

"Stop teasing me. I want to feel your mouth wrapped around my dick," he said reaching for the waistband of his shorts to push them down. He felt a light touch on his hand to stop him.

"I'm running this show," she said throwing him a devilish grin.

She lifted each foot and removed his shoes. She reached in the back pockets of his jeans before discarding them and slowly moved up his body. She made sure her hardened nipples brushed every part of him she could.

Dylan sucked in his breath and reached for her. When she stepped out of his reach he frowned and had to fight the urge to growl in frustration. His dick was throbbing, standing out in front of him and only she could take the ache away.

"Sasha," he began.

"All things in due time," she said putting her fingers to his lips to keep him from continuing.

She reached for his hand and led him forward until she was backed up against his desk. She turned her back to him briefly while she cleared a space. Seeing an opportunity he couldn't resist Dylan gently pushed her forward and allowed his dick to find the heated crease between her legs. He moved cautiously all too aware he was on the edge of bursting. When she looked at him over her shoulder, a smile played around the edges of her mouth, he almost came right then. This is how he wanted to take her, from behind with her arms splayed out in front of her and the heavy desk allowing no escape. Dylan was about to voice that wish when Sasha placed a gentle hand on his bare chest and pushed, causing him to step back so she could turn around to face him once again.

Dylan stood watching, his dick still throbbing with unfulfilled need, as Sasha began undressing in front of him. Dear Lord was she trying to kill him? He watched as if in a trance as more of her golden brown skin appeared. She slowly tugged her shirt from the waist of her jeans and pulled it over her head. Inch by glorious inch more skin was exposed until bare pert breasts appeared. She threw her shirt over his shoulder to join his clothes on the floor before she unbuttoned her jeans, giving a little wiggle to get them down her hips. The scrap of material shielding her prized treasure was all that remained.

Knowing what she wanted before she asked for it, Dylan placed strong hands at her waist and lifted her onto the surface of his desk.

"Oh that's cold," she said in surprise as the cool surface of the desk met her heated skin.

Changing the Rules

"Don't worry I think I can warm you up," he said moving between her open legs, his dick seeking the heat and moisture of her pussy.

"I have no doubts that you will."

Sasha placed the heels of her feet on the edge of the desk, causing her pussy to open around the thin material between her legs. She then reached down and moved the material to the side allowing him to see the moisture running from her pussy.

"Would you like to come in?" she asked as she began to slowly run a finger across her clit, causing it to harden.

Dylan couldn't believe how he throbbed at the sight before him. He licked his dry lips and pushed down his shorts before stepping closer. She handed him the condom she'd obviously retrieved from his pants pocket. As quick as possible he opened the packet and sheathed it over his throbbing dick. Task done he placed the head of his aching member at her opening and pushed only enough to get the head wet. Her mouth opened and her eyes were glazed over in desire. When he pushed a little more he heard her gasp. He pulled completely out and stroked himself along the length of his shaft. A soft chuckle met his ears.

"So I see it's your turn to play games. Well, that's okay. I learned a few last night myself," she said and thrust two fingers into her hot cavern.

With each stroke of her fingers he heard her breathing become more labored signaling she was close to her peak. When she pulled out glistening fingers he reached for her hand and lifted them to his mouth. Dylan sucked her nectar drenched fingers deep into his hot mouth as he shoved his throbbing dick into her heated pussy.

"Oh Dylan," Sasha gasped as he filled her.

The height of the desk allowed him the perfect opportunity to sink every inch of his dick into her eager pussy. But still it wasn't enough. The more he stroked the more he wanted. Leaning down he drew her hardened nipples into his mouth and sucked. He felt the clenching of her cunt muscles around his dick. She was close.

"Oh God Dylan. I'm gonna cum," she gasped as he felt her pussy tighten like a vice around the length of his dick.

Dylan held steady as her orgasm moved through her. When her breathing had slowed he began thrusting into her again. Slower this time. Teasing them both. He felt his balls tighten against the base of his dick. Each stroke brought him closer to his orgasm but still it wasn't enough. He wanted … he knew what he wanted and how he wanted it. Suddenly he pulled out of her. Dylan pulled Sasha up from the desk and turned her around so her back faced him and the fronts of her thighs were braced against the cool wood of his desk.

She wiggled her ass against his pulsing dick. He gripped the sides of her hips to keep her still. He wanted to be inside of her when he came and if she kept this up he'd shoot his load now and that was not what he wanted. Pulling the sides of her ass far apart he poked her anus with his dick before allowing his swollen member to find its way to her heated center. He slipped slowly inside allowing a sigh to leave his lips as her tight pussy walls closed around him once more.

"Oh Sasha you have the sweetest pussy."

A groan of pleasure was her reply as he began to thrust within her tight confines. Dylan couldn't believe how tight she felt from this position. The walls of pussy felt like a vice grip on his dick as he slowly moved in and out of her increasing his speed until he heard the fronts of his thighs smacking against the backs of hers. The sounds and scent of sex filled the room as he continued to slam into her from behind. Dylan threw his head back and gave a groan of pleasure as he felt his balls tighten further against his body.

"Oh God Sasha I'm gonna cum. I want you to cum with me."

Her breathless answer came in between gasps for air.

"Oh yes. I'm almost there. So close. I can feel it. Fuck me harder."

Dylan pulled out until just the tip of his dick was inserted in her hot pussy and shoved back in until he was buried deeper than he'd ever been. When his dick hit the back wall of her pussy he gave a shout as his load shot through the length of his dick.

Sasha continued to move against him until he heard her own shout of release and felt her pussy began to convulse around his dick, causing another wave of cum to be released from his member.

A slow satisfied smile turned up the corners of his mouth. He kissed Sasha's bare shoulder.

"How am I ever supposed to get any work done in this office again?" he asked lifting his sweat drenched body away from hers. He pulled slowly from the confines of her body and turned her around to face him.

Pushing her braids back from her face Sasha gave him a cheeky grin.

"Hmm, I don't know but I'm sure you'll have fun thinking about what did get done in this office," she said and reached down between their bodies. She removed the used condom, throwing it in the trashcan beside Dylan's desk.

"Come on let's go see what other rooms we can christen," she said reaching up to give him a quick kiss before she grabbed his hand and pulled him naked out of his office.

Chapter 16

Sasha leaned back in her chair and waited for the printer to stop. She stood up and stretched muscles that had been confined too long in one position. Glancing over at the clock on her desk she realized it was later than she'd thought. She had dinner plans with Dylan scheduled for seven and it was six forty now. Hmm, she thought as she reached for her desk phone. Why hadn't he called her? All week he'd been tied up in meetings and conference calls. Last week hadn't been much better. She'd barely seen him except for when she left the building in the evenings and he took a break to walk her to her car. There had been more canceled plans over the last two weeks than not. She hoped tonight wouldn't be another cancellation.

"Matthews." Came the gruff reply from the other end.

"Are we still on for dinner?" Sasha asked sensing something was wrong from the way he answered the phone.

She heard the deep exhale of breath on the other end. Yep looked like she'd be eating dinner alone again.

"Hey sweetheart. I meant to call you earlier to see if we could postpone until later or reschedule. I'm in the middle of reviewing the budget for the company we just bought in California and I'm having all kinds of problems with their figures."

She could feel his frustration coming through the phone.

"That's okay so what time do you think you're gonna be done? Maybe I can stop by and give you a hand," she asked shutting down her computer.

A pause came from the other end.

"I'd love nothing better, but the last time we worked in the same office we got little work done," he said laughter in his voice.

She recalled that as well. Okay so maybe that wouldn't be the most beneficial idea for getting the budget reviewed.

"How come you're looking at the numbers? Not to sound like a snob but aren't you a little too important for tedious stuff like that?" she asked debating on whether or not she should boot her computer back up. She had work she could do while she waited for him.

When another deep laugh came through the phone, Sasha braced her hands against her desk. The sound immediately caused tingles in her stomach.

"Normally I wouldn't. We had one of our other people looking at it but when things began to look a little funny it found its way to my desk for a closer review. So as of now anything dealing with funds for that office comes to me. I may end up taking a trip to San Diego to find out exactly how things are being run. It's a mess."

"That bad huh? How late do you think you'll be?"

"I don't know. I may be here for a while yet. I'm sorry baby I was really looking forward to seeing you tonight," he said his voice having dropped.

Sasha sat back down in her chair and allowed his voice to wash over her weary body. She'd been looking forward to tonight as well. It had been almost a month since they'd spent that first weekend together. Since then they'd spent as much time together as they could manage getting to know each other's minds and bodies. She enjoyed their long talks at night when conflicting schedules made it difficult for them to see each other but they'd never gone this long before. It had been three days since they'd made love under the stars Sunday night on Dylan's balcony and her body was aching for his.

"I was too but I understand," she said resigning herself to another sleepless night.

"If I work late for the rest of this week I may be able to take the weekend off."

Changing the Rules

"Don't push it. I understand if we don't see each other this weekend."

She tried not to let the disappointment she felt come through in her words but she didn't know if she'd been successful. She missed him terribly and wanted to see him.

"It's not okay dammit. I've barely seen you in the last two weeks except for the brief reprieve I get in the evenings. It's not enough."

Amen, she thought. Her body seconded the motion. The same frustration she heard coming from him was running through her veins right now. All she'd thought about all day was that they'd be alone after dinner and she would be able to touch him and be touched by him. Then a thought hit her.

"Look why don't I order you something to eat since you're gonna be here a little longer. What would you like?"

"You a-la-carte," came the husky answer from the other end.

"I'll see if they have that on the menu," she said and hung up the phone.

The smile playing around the corners of her mouth could only be called mischievous. Sasha could hardly believe she was thinking what she was thinking. It was way out of character for her, but then so was having an affair with a white man. But this, this was really out there. Could she pull it off? She grabbed her keys and pocketbook from her desk and left her office. There was only one way to find out.

***

Dylan was sitting at his desk, his head thrown back, eyes closed. He was waiting for the throbbing in his neck and head to ease before he went back to work. It had been almost an hour since he'd gotten off the phone with Sasha and he hadn't made any progress. Thoughts of what he was missing plagued him. This is not how he'd envisioned their courtship going. He had wanted to wine and dine her, make her realize they were no different other than the color of their skin. And he'd been successful in doing that until now. This new company they'd acquired was stressing out everyone in the company and now it had fallen squarely on his shoulders for resolution. He'd hoped to avoid a trip to California but as he looked over the scattered pages of the spreadsheet he didn't see any way around it. As it was it was taking up more of his time than he'd expected it to. He toyed briefly with the idea of asking Sasha to go with him. But he quickly discarded the idea. He didn't want to raise any suspicions in the office about their relationship until she was ready.

He ran agitated fingers through his hair as he thought back on the amount of time he'd missed out on with Sasha over the past few weeks. He knew she was busy with a huge new client and was working late into the evening herself, but it still bothered him. Just as he'd found a woman he wanted to spend every available minute with this had to happen. Now here he was looking at being out of town for a week or maybe even longer. He knew Sasha was still unsure about where their relationship was headed and he hoped this wouldn't cost him points he'd already earned.

Knock. Knock.

Who could that be? Carla would have left hours ago, he thought looking over at the clock. Then he recalled Sasha's offer to order him something for dinner. It had been awhile since he'd last eaten.

"Come in," he called out wondering what she'd ordered him.

He was surprised at the sight of Sasha standing in his doorway. God she was the best food for his eyes. He got up from the desk and approached her, a smile on his face.

"God sweetheart you are a sight for tired eyes. I missed you," he said pulling her close to him. She felt so good in his arms,

Small arms came around his waist to embrace him in return.

"I missed you too. I didn't think it was possible to miss someone as much as I have you, but I was wrong," she said pulling slightly away, leaning back against the strong arms still wrapped around her waist.

Gazing down into her beautiful brown eyes Dylan smiled at the simple joy he felt just by holding her. He pulled her to him again and felt the rough material of her coat against his hands. Why was she wearing a coat? It had topped off at ninety degrees today in Chicago. The temperature couldn't have dropped that low since he'd last checked. He was about to ask the reason for the coat when he noticed the tops of her breasts pushed against the confines of the coat. He looked closer at her small breasts and couldn't detect any confines. Surely she hadn't. Not his sensible Sasha. Dylan dropped his arms from her waist and stepped back. Was that uncertainty in her eyes? Looking closer he distinctly got the impression she was nervous.

"Sasha why do you have on a trench coat?" he asked, his dick already throbbed within the confines of his pants at the thought of the possibility of her being naked under that coat.

She lowered her head before lifting her sparkling eyes to meet his.

"I brought you dinner," she said and began slowly unbuttoning her coat.

Changing the Rules

With each button she undid Dylan's dick grew harder. With each inch of brown skin she uncovered his heart skipped another beat. When she stood before him with her coat wide open for him to see her naked body his brain stopped functioning. Dear god. His hungry eyes devoured every inch of her from her beautiful upturned breasts with dark nipples poking out to greet him to her downy bush hiding her treasures. His tongue came out to lick his dry lips in anticipation. He followed her naked glory down her flat stomach to her well toned legs to the high heels she had on her feet. He'd told her he loved a woman in heels, especially one with nice legs like hers. She'd accommodated him every day since. Now as he looked down at her red high heels he felt a bead of perspiration running down his neck. She was beautiful and she was offering herself to him. Maybe he hadn't lost any ground. He couldn't imagine the Sasha he'd interviewed ever prancing around Chicago in nothing but a coat and red high heels.

Chapter 17

The nervousness Sasha had felt entering the building was slowly subsiding to be replaced by a strong desire to be ravished by the gorgeous man standing in front of her. After she'd gotten off the phone with Dylan she'd done something she'd always fantasized of doing. She'd left the building, driven to the closest clothing store and purchased a long trench coat. Her practical side had made sure it was a good quality coat she would wear again, but still she'd done something she'd never thought she had the nerve to do. Coming back to her office she'd slowly undressed, the whole time debating with her better senses over what she was about to do. Never before had she met a man who had brought out the adventurous side of her. Hell she hadn't known she'd had one before meeting Dylan Matthews.

Since meeting him and entering into a sexual relationship with him she'd had sex in more places than she'd ever imagined. Not one room in either of their homes had been safe when it came to their desire for each other.

Changing the Rules

Memories of Dylan fucking her senseless came unchecked to her mind and Sasha brought her hand up to cover her heavy breasts. She caressed them, longing for it to be his hands pulling and tugging at her puckered nipples. Soon she told herself as she lifted her gaze to stare into the beautiful blue eyes of the man staring intently at her. Her coat fell from her shoulders into a puddle on the floor. She stood before him in all her naked glory proud of her petite stature and the small perky breasts growing heavier the longer he started at her. Never before had she been as aware of her affect on a man as she was with Dylan.

She allowed her gaze to take in the sight of him. His shirt sleeves were rolled up to his elbows, the top three buttons of his dress shirt undone, displaying the dark dusting of chest hairs, his dark chestnut hair looked as if he'd been running his fingers through it all day. It had grown since she'd first seen him that day in the elevator. No longer was it simply grazing the collar of his shirt it was beyond that point now and she found it sexy as hell.

"I think you're a little over dressed. Don't you?" she asked moving closer and began undressing him.

"I would say so. Honey what if someone had stopped you on your way up here? You didn't have on any clothes."

Sasha merely smiled at him, standing on tiptoes to push his shirt off his broad shoulders. Even in her heels he was still a considerable bit taller than she was.

"Oh don't be such an old maid," she said laughing at the look on his face. She laughed even harder when she saw him mouth the words "old maid".

"I wasn't dressed like this when I came back in the building. I had on my clothes and undressed in my office. Happy?" she asked crouching down to undo his pants, careful of the growing bulge springing out to greet her.

"Not quite," he said catching her hair up in his hands and pushing her mouth towards his dick.

"Well, let's see what we can do about that," she replied.

Dylan stepped out of his shoes and pants balancing his hands on her slim shoulders until he stood naked before her except for his socks. She looked up and noticed his gaze was fixed on her.

"Tell me what you want," she said stroking the length of him.

"I want you to suck my dick like only you can," came the quick response.

He placed his hand at the back of her head holding her welcoming mouth in place over his dick. Sasha took him in the warm cavern of her mouth where she loved him up and down his steadily growing length. Reaching up to cup his balls in the palms of her hands she relaxed her throat and took him deep. The groan Dylan let out was worth the discomfort she felt at having her airways restricted. Soon she was able to take him further with only pleasure meeting each mouthful of hard flesh.

"Sasha. Oh god, I'm gonna cum. Can you take it all sweetheart?" Dylan asked moving his dick in and out of her mouth.

She allowed him to pop free from her warm depths, licking the veins in the sides of his impressive length.

"I don't know," she said grazing his head lightly with her teeth. She felt the shiver run through him. "Let's see shall we."

Immediately his dick disappeared within the confines of her mouth once again. Flattening her tongue, the swollen head of his dick slid effortlessly down the back of her throat followed by another half an inch. She pulled her head back and began to use more pressure along the length of him, using the cavern of her mouth to imitate how it would feel once he got inside her aching pussy.

"Oh Sasha. I'm gonna cum sweetheart."

His fingers wrapped tightly in her hair as he began moving his dick in and out of her mouth with more force.

Sasha relaxed her throat and allowed him to fuck her mouth as she squeezed his balls. She felt them tighten further in her hands and knew he was close. The first shot of hot cum hit her tonsils and it took everything for her to not react and gag on his dick. Another hot shot quickly followed by a gush of cum washing the back walls of her mouth as she felt Dylan shaking with the power of his orgasm.

Once the last drop had been drained from his still hard dick she released him from her mouth licking him from base to tip once more before rising. Her mouth was quickly taken in a harsh kiss that took the breath from her. She felt Dylan's tongue sweeping the insides of her mouth tasting himself on her tongue. The kiss was over as quickly as it began. He lifted her in his arms and walked the short distance to the couch.

Sasha had barely caught her breath when she felt her legs being spread and Dylan's tongue grazing against her aching clit.

"Ahh Dylan."

Over and over again he licked her clit until it became as hard as the nipples he was pinching. He moved to her open gushing hole where he shoved his tongue in and began lapping up the sweet nectar running unchecked from between her legs. The pleasure running through her was too much. She felt the pressure building in the pit of her stomach. As Dylan began fucking her pussy with his tongue she moved her fingers between her legs and stroked her clit. The pressure built and finally burst when he shoved two fingers into her depths. Her orgasm came hard and fast, but he wasn't done yet. He pushed her legs together over her head, effectively baring her pussy and her little brown hole to his gaze. He licked the escaping juices from her pussy to her anus where he paid special attention. Being in a position of limited movement Sasha could only thrash her head back and forth on the couch as he continued his assault on her pussy and ass. She felt a finger slowly enter her asshole and lifted her ass off the couch.

"Harder Dylan. I want you to shove it in harder. It feels so good," she gasped as she felt the pressure in her stomach building again.

Two fingers in her pussy joined the finger in her ass and he shoved them in and out causing wave after wave of pleasure to flow through her as another orgasm took her.

"I want you to fuck me now," she screamed. His fingers were okay but Sasha wanted him buried deep within her. She wanted him to fuck her.

"Don't worry that was the plan," he said his voice thick with desire.

Sindee Lynn

Sasha gasped when he pulled his fingers from within her depths, grazing the sides of her walls in her ass and pussy. She watched through lowered lashes as he briefly left her to retrieve his pants for the roll of condoms he'd taken to carrying around with him. A groan tore from her throat when he gripped his dick and began stroking himself. He was so hot and he was all hers.

Reaching her side, he leaned down and stroked the tops of her thighs until she opened them for him. He kneeled for a moment between them just gazing at her pussy before he pushed into her in one stroke. Her body spread wide from the width of him and she could only lay there panting for air as he continued to drive into her.

"Oh yes Dylan. That's it. I want you to fuck me."

"You wanna be fucked huh?" he asked pulling his length out until just the head was inside.

Sasha lifted her ass up off the couch trying to bring him back.

"Yes dammit," she yelled. "I want you to fuck me."

"Your wish is my command," he said and slammed his dick into her hitting the back wall of her hot and ready hole. She screamed at the pain and pleasure of it. The pleasure of having him slamming over and over into her caused shivers to spread through her body. Her orgasm built until she felt hot cum gushing from her depths.

Changing the Rules

"Oh god Dylan I'm cumming,"

A grunt was her only response as she felt him begin to shake and shiver on top of her as his own orgasm hit him.

***

"Man, I'll never be able to look at this couch the same again," Dylan said laughing as he stroked Sasha's naked shoulder.

Soft laughter filled his ears as she reached up to kiss him on his cheek. The tenderness of her actions made his heart ache.

"Forget the couch. I'll never be able to walk in your office again without remembering this whole night," she said snuggling closer.

He reached for her coat he'd retrieved earlier from the floor. He threw it over their naked bodies to keep the chill off as their body temperatures came back to normal from sizzling.

"I hope I didn't put you too far off schedule."

The concern in her voice touched another part of his heart and brought a smile to his face.

"I'll take interruptions like this one anytime besides I wasn't getting much done. It seems thoughts of a pint sized woman kept running through my head and I couldn't clear it to think."

"Yeah? I bet she wasn't naked in a trench coat," she said laughing.

Dylan had to laugh too because he would never have thought Sasha would do something like this.

"No I must admit she wasn't. So I like reality a whole lot better."

He paused, not sure how to bring up what he wanted to say next.

"Sasha?"

"Hmm," came the drowsy reply.

"I was wondering if you would like to accompany me to a party at the mayor's mansion."

Dylan held his breath as he waited for her reply. He'd declined several offers for parties in the last couple of weeks, not wanting to attend without her by his side. But this one was different. The mayor and his wife were personal friends of his. Besides he wanted them to meet Sasha. It was the perfect opportunity to introduce her into his world.

"The mayor of Chicago?" came the hesitant reply.

"None other. He's been a client of Presco for several years and we've been friends just as long. He and his wife are celebrating their thirty-fifth wedding anniversary."

Changing the Rules

Dylan didn't know how to take the silence. He could practically hear her mind working overtime.

"Is it formal attire?" she finally asked.

"Yes."

More silence. He had already decided if she said no he would make his apologies and not attend himself. He wasn't in the mood to be put upon by a bunch of women he had no interest in.

"When is it?"

"Two weeks from Saturday."

Another long pause followed.

"I guess that means I'll have to go shopping."

Relief and joy washed over him. He hugged her close. He knew it hadn't been an easy decision for her to make but the fact she'd made it gave him hope that soon she'd be ready to make another decision. To have him in her life permanently.

***

Click. Click. Click.

"Well, well, well who do we have here? I don't believe I've ever seen your pretty little face before."

He readjusted the lens of his camera to get a clearer view. A smile spread across a deeply tanned face. Hours hiding out waiting for that perfect shot with the sun beating down on you could do that to a person. But he didn't mind as long as the payoff in the end was a big one and he'd just stumbled upon a gold mine. He hadn't been back in a few weeks but something had told him to take a chance. He'd learned early on to listen to his instincts. It had cost him a c-note to get in here tonight. His regular guy hadn't been working. But man had it ever paid off for him.

He'd tried to tell them Dylan Matthews was not a dried up cash cow. Sure he'd been off the scene for awhile. But he'd been following him for years and knew there had to be a reason. Maybe this woman was it. He had seen the different women he always had on his arm. All of them had been beautiful but definitely not the warmest of women. They'd all held the same cold calculating look in their eyes even when smiling pretty for the cameras. He couldn't recall there ever being a black woman before. Though he could tell by the way Matthews was holding and touching her she was different. She couldn't be more than five feet four or five inches in height. Compared to Matthews' bulking six feet three, petite was an understatement. He adjusted the long range scope on his camera to get a clearer look. Yeah this one was special.

He watched as the two lovers gave each other one final passion filled kiss. Geez he could practically feel the heat from where he sat.

Changing the Rules

"Man Matthews you got it bad for this one," he commented seeing the way he caressed her face before finally leaving her side. Matthews left the same way they'd come down, the private elevator that led directly to the executive's only garage under Presco.

He gently placed his camera on the seat beside him and started his engine.

"Now let's go find out who this mystery woman is."

He pulled out of the garage following his next big pay check.

Chapter 18

The smile on Sasha's face when she walked into the Presco building on Monday morning was brighter than normal. She had spent the entire weekend with Dylan at his place. He'd decided he'd put enough time into the financials and not enough time into her. A flush of heat sufficed her face as she recalled how much attention he'd given her this weekend. She didn't think there was a spot on her body that had been left undiscovered or unlicked.

Stepping out of the elevator and heading for her office, she smiled a greeting at the people she passed in the hall. She barely noticed the odd looks she was getting or the strained expressions. She shook it off as she continued to her office. Maybe she was imagining it because they weren't seeing the world through the same rose tinted glasses she was.

"Good Morning Violet," Sasha greeted their department secretary as she passed her desk. When the secretary only grunted back a reply she paused. That was odd. She turned and walked back to Violet.

Changing the Rules

"Everything okay this morning," she asked concern in her voice.

Violet had been nothing but friendly and helpful when she'd joined the department. Now could possibly be her opportunity to return the favor.

"Oh everything's just fine Ms. Jordan," Violet said a twist to her lips and sarcasm in her tone.

A frown puckered Sasha's forehead as she stood gazing down at the woman behind the desk. She was about to question her further when her cell phone rang. She turned from the secretary promising herself she would get to the bottom of whatever her problem was before the end of the day. If she had done something to offend her she wanted to make it right.

"Hello."

"Are you in your office?" Cat's voice came across the line.

"I just got here why?"

A sigh came across the line.

"Have you by chance seen the paper this morning?"

There was something in Cat's voice she couldn't quite figure out. She put her stuff down on her desk and closed her door.

"Not yet why?"

Another sigh came across the line. A feeling of apprehension caused a knot to form in Sasha's stomach.

"Cat what's going on?"

"Are you sitting down?"

Sasha instantly fell into her chair. Something was wrong she knew it now. Cat never hedged. She was always direct and to the point. Something terrible had happened.

"What is it Cat? What's happened? You're freaking me out. Is it B.J.? Is she okay?"

"B.J.'s fine. As least as far as I know. I need you to look in the paper."

Moving stuff around on her desk, she couldn't find the stack of newspapers that were always there waiting for her every morning. She got up and checked outside her door. She bent down and picked them up. Because of her job there were always at least three different newspapers.

"Okay, I got them. Which financial section of what newspaper should I be looking at," Sasha asked.

Maybe this was about the stocks she'd recommended Cat invest in. God Sasha hoped they hadn't tanked or anything. She'd done her research well before recommending them.

"Not the financials section. The society page of the local paper," Cat said.

Changing the Rules

Her stomach bottomed out. The society page. Quickly pushing the other newspapers to the floor until she found the Chicago Tribune, she noticed her fingers were trembling.

"What am I looking for?"

"You'll know when you see it."

Sasha flipped through the different sections until she had no doubts she'd reached the right page. Her mouth dropped open and her cell phone fell out of her lifeless fingers. On the front page of the society page was a picture of her and Dylan in the private parking garage in what could only be described as a lover's embrace. In fact that's how the reporter had described it. Her mind moved back in time to when the picture was taken. It had to have been on Wednesday night when Dylan had walked her to her car. The night she'd shown up in nothing but a trench coat … oh dear God. Sasha guessed she should be lucky whoever had taken the picture had gotten it after she'd put her clothes back on.

Ring… ring….

Sasha glanced at her desk phone. Should she answer it? It was no telling who the hell it could be. Thank god her parents lived in Florida. But B.J. oh shit. The ringing stopped only briefly before it began again.

Ring… ring...

Trembling fingers picked up the receiver.

"Sasha Jordan." Please oh please don't let it be B.J. Not right now.

"What the hell is going on Sasha?"

Sasha felt like banging her head on her desk as her sister's angry voice came through the phone lines.

"I take it you saw the newspaper?"

"Uh yeah I saw it. All of Chicago is looking at it right now. Who the hell is this man to you? And more importantly why didn't you tell me?"

What could she say? Her head was about to explode. So many thoughts. Confusion. It all pressed down on her. She couldn't do this right now. She needed to talk to Dylan.

"Look B.J. I can't talk right now," Sasha said panic preparing to set in.

"Sasha ….," B.J. began.

"B.J.," Sasha yelled into the phone. "I can't do this right now. I will call you back," she said and hung up the phone.

No sooner had she put the phone back on its hook that it began ringing again. Oh god Sasha thought. She couldn't breathe. She stood up behind her desk and took huge gulps of air. How could this have happened? How could she have let this happen? This is what she had wanted to avoid at all costs. Now it all made sense. The stares people had been giving her this morning. She'd foolishly thought they were wondering at the goofy grin on her face. But they'd been looking at her for entirely different reasons. She recalled Violet's odd behavior this morning.

"Oh God," she whispered.

She needed to talk to Dylan.

Sasha practically ran from her office, cursing the high heels she had begun to wear everyday because Dylan liked them. Dammit she had been such a fool. She had changed her life for him. And this is what it had gotten her. While waiting for the elevator to come she tried to ignore the odd looks of those who passed her in the hallway. She tapped her foot impatiently.

"Come on," she said punching the button again.

The doors finally whisked open and she collided with a hard body.

"Excuse me," she said glancing up into the concerned blue gaze of the man she'd been on her way to see.

"Anytime you'd like to bump into me is my pleasure," he said an uncertain smile on his face.

Sasha didn't find the humor.

"I was on my way to see you. Have you seen the newspapers this morning?" she asked her anger over the situation coming to the forefront now that she had someone to direct it at.

"Yeah I saw it. That's why I was on my way to see you. I wanted to see how you were doing."

How she was doing? Sasha wanted to yell at the top of her lungs that she wasn't doing well at all. Gazing up at him she didn't see the same concern that was coursing through her. Why wasn't he as upset about this as she was? Then it hit her. He was used to his face being plastered all over the newspaper. It was no big deal for him. He wouldn't have to worry about people wondering how he got his job. He was used to being the subject of gossip. But that was not something she was used to nor did she want to get used to it.

"How am I doing Dylan? Well, let's see. My picture is plastered on the front page of the society section. Every client I have is looking at that this morning. My family and friends are looking at that this morning. The people in this office have obviously already seen it," she said looking around them at the people who were moving entirely too slow around them to be doing anything other than eavesdropping on their conversation.

Dylan's gaze darkened as he took in the meandering people around them.

"Doesn't anyone have any work to do on this floor?" he asked.

The scurry of employees moving on their way almost brought a smile to Sasha's face. But it only served to remind her of Dylan's position in the company and that no matter how you sliced it, he was her boss.

"Sasha I've been in touch with the newspaper to find out how the picture could have been taken in our private parking garage. I made sure to remind them the photographer was trespassing on private property and that is a crime. There'll be an apology in tomorrow's paper. So you see it'll blow over shortly," he said reaching for her.

She put her hands up to ward him off. The last thing she wanted him to do was touch her.

"You don't understand. That all happens tomorrow. People are looking at the pictures today. And they've already started speculating."

"So let them. We were eventually gonna make our relationship known anyway. I would have preferred it be on our terms and not like this but what's done is done."

In a calmer moment she may have agreed with his rationale. They had planned to bring their relationship into the light. But none of that mattered right now when the looks on the faces of the people she'd passed this morning and the coolness in the greeting from Violet all said one thing. That she, an outsider, had gotten her job because she'd slept with the CFO of the company.

Hot tears burned the backs of her eyes. It was happening again. This time she'd walked right into it with her eyes wide open. How could she have been so stupid? She'd stepped outside her rules and now she was paying the price for it.

"As long as we face all of this together and people see we're not ashamed of what we have. It should be okay."

When she glanced up he was shaking his head. It was if he knew what she was about to say. She saw the pleading in his eyes.

"Dylan I don't think it's a good idea for us to see each other any longer."

He reached for her hands. "Sasha don't do this. We both know why you got this job. Your qualifications speak for themselves along with the results and comments of your clients. You're perfect for this job and for me. Take some time to think about it. Don't make a decision you might regret later."

The pleading in his tone almost had her changing her mind. The misery clearly reflected in his blue gaze threatened to crumble her resolve. But it was time for her to stop living in a fantasy world. This was reality. And the reality was that her reputation at this company was now tarnished. It was time for her to take control once again of where she was going instead of just being along for the ride. She gently tugged her hands from his warm grasp.

"The only decision I regret is not listening to my better judgment. Good bye Dylan."

Sasha turned and walked back to her office. Tears clogged her throat. She somehow managed to hold them back until she was behind her closed door. Sliding down until her bottom hit the floor she buried her face in her hands. The ringing telephone on her desk faded into the background as she allowed her pain and misery to swallow her whole. The problem was she didn't know if she cried for the injustice she felt over the invasion into her privacy or over the passion that would be forever reflected in the black and white copy. A passion she feared she'd never have again.

Chapter 19

"Okay so what are we gonna do about Sasha?" B.J. asked the group of women gathered in her living room.

Cat glanced at B.J. The deep lines of concern reflected on her face matched those of the women around her. B.J. had called an emergency intervention meeting after she'd made another failed attempt at getting through to Sasha. Something had to be done and soon. Sasha had kept herself confined within her house for the last two weeks. The only place she went was work where she didn't sometimes leave until nine or ten o'clock at night. She was on a mission to prove herself worthy of the job she'd been given. In Cat's opinion the only person she had to prove anything to was herself. She'd tried to tell Sasha that but she like everyone else had failed.

"What can we do? She won't talk to any of us" Safari Lawson said taking a sip of her wine. "Hell it's like she wants to pretend it never happened."

"That's exactly what she's trying to do Ri. That's how Sasha has always coped with stuff she can't handle.

Changing the Rules

She tries to ignore it and hopes it'll go away," B.J. said taking a seat beside Safari on her couch.

"Even after the apology they ran, which shocked the hell out of me, she's still not talking about it. It's been almost two weeks since the picture ran and things have died down," Lynn Sanders said.

The look of concern on her face could only be described as that of a mother watching one of her kids. Lynn was the oldest in their close knit group of friends. No one who ever met her believed she was forty-five. She almost always had to pull out her id to show them.

"They ran the retraction because Presco threatened to sue their sorry asses, I'm sure. The picture was taken on private property. How stupid can you get," Nicole Johnson exclaimed from the chair beside Cat.

Cat had to agree it was a stupid move on the part of the photographer and the person at the newspaper who made the bad judgment call to run the photos. She'd had a helluva time convincing Dylan that it would not benefit him whatsoever to go to the newspaper office for a face to face confrontation with the photographer.

"Yeah well I hope they fired the guy who let him in that night. It's as much his fault as it is the photographer who took the pictures," Safari said.

Dylan had taken care of that too. In fact it had been the first thing he'd done. Four people had lost their jobs at Presco because of this. The guy who had been on duty that night had implicated others. They'd all been fired.

"You're awful quiet Cat. You got any professional thoughts on all of this?" Nicole asked her.

All eyes were on her. Cat hated this. Everyone always assumed she had the answer to every problem that arose because she was a psychiatrist. Didn't they know when it was personal it made it ten times harder to be objective? She'd come to think of Dylan as a friend in the past months and felt trapped in the middle. She understood his frustration over Sasha's continued refusal to speak with him but her heart went out to her best friend who couldn't even see that it didn't have to be this way. That's what she got for meddling.

"In my professional opinion I believe that for Sasha to avoid her problems instead of dealing with them is unhealthy," Cat said rising from her chair. "As her friend, I think she needs to grow the hell up and learn to face her problems."

Cat headed towards B.J.'s bar. She needed a drink.

"You don't think that this guy, Dylan Matthews, should bare some of the blame?" B.J. asked. "What if he took advantage of her?"

Cat rolled her eyes in the back of her head but kept quiet.

"Aw come on B.J. How do you take advantage of a grown woman really?" Nicole said shaking her head in disagreement to B.J.'s words.

"Besides it's not like he's the janitor and she didn't know who he was. He's the CFO of the company," Safari quickly added.

"Sasha would have known who he was. Hell I know who he is and I don't work for Presco. His face has been all over the place for some reason or other," Nicole continued. "No she knew what she was getting into."

"I have to agree with them. Sasha is a thinker. She would have rationally weighed the pros and cons of this relationship or whatever it is she has with him before she made a move," Lynn added.

"Hmph, pros and cons. Did you get a good look at him? I don't think there are any cons. Dylan Matthews is gorgeous. Maybe that's what Sasha was thinking about. Hell who can blame her," Safari said shaking her head.

"Not I girl," Nicole said in agreement reaching over to high five Safari.

When the two began to discuss Dylan's many attributes Cat couldn't keep the smile from her face. Sasha had worried with indecision on whether or not to tell their friends. Cat hadn't been able to convince her it wouldn't have mattered to any of them one way or the other.

"Ladies we are getting a little off subject here," Lynn said glancing towards B.J.

Cat looked over at B.J. from where she stood mixing her drink. Well maybe it would have mattered to one of them. Irritation could clearly be seen on B.J.'s face over the jokes Safari and Nicole were making. Cat's professional side said there was something deeper going on here than what was on the surface. Her other side, the one that had just finished meddling, told it to shut the hell up.

"Does anyone know how long this has been going on?" Lynn asked bringing them back to the subject at hand.

"I know I didn't get the memo. I would have definitely have read this one if I had," Safari said still laughing.

"Yeah I think we all would have. Who would have ever thought it possible? Our Sasha with a white man. Hell it's certainly newsworthy," Nicole said laughing along with Safari.

"Well I fail to see the humor in this. I don't understand what Sasha could have been thinking. And Dylan Matthews… what was he thinking to have let this happen?" B.J. asked. Anger flashed in her eyes and was evident in her body language.

"No one let this happen? Some jerk of a photographer paid a parking attendant to gain access to a private parking garage." Cat said walking back to her seat, drink in hand.

"Yes well if it hadn't been this it would have been something else. Sasha should have used better judgment than to get involved with a man like him," B.J. replied.

What the hell did that mean? A man like him. Cat felt her resolve not to be too vocal in tonight's meeting fading.

"So what …….Sasha should have sat around and been bored to tears with Louis the next door neighbor. That guy is a walking talking advertisement for hemorrhoid cream," Cat responded shaking her head in disbelief.

"It would have been better than being made to look like a cheap office fling for your boss. He's probably moved on to the next conquest by now. You won't see him worrying about who's talking behind his back."

"I'm sorry I thought we were talking about Dylan not Melvin."

Cat heard the gasps of her friends at the mention of Sasha's ex-fiancé. It was as if his name was the foulest thing that could be said.

"I can't tell the difference. Where the hell has Dylan been during this whole thing?" B.J. fired back.

"You wanna know where Dylan has been? He's been threatening to smash in the face of the photographer who took the picture and the editor who approved the running. He's been getting people fired. And more importantly, he's been begging Sasha every day to listen to reason and not to let something like this ruin everything they have."

"Just whose side are you on here Cat? You're supposed to be Sasha's best friend and you sound like you're taking his side. You also sound like you know a whole lot more than you've been letting on," B.J. practically spit the words at Cat.

Cat closed her eyes and prayed for a calm she was far from feeling. It was always this way between her and B.J. especially where Sasha was concerned. Even had she not been a professional she could have diagnosed B.J.'s jealousy a mile away. She shook her head and took a deep breath. The next time she felt the need to meddle in someone else life she would definitely think on things a little longer than she had for this one.

"I'm not trying to take sides B.J. But it's hard to be in Sasha's corner when she's not even standing there herself."

Cat stared at B.J. daring her to deny her words.

"Okay I think we all need to calm down," Safari said from the couch glancing between Cat and B.J. "And if Cat knows more than any of us, I think we can pretty much figure out why."

Cat didn't know if that was a compliment or a backhanded slap in the face because of her dating preferences. Whatever it was she was glad it diverted any further questions about how much she actually knew about the situation.

"Look B.J. I know you may not wanna hear this but when I saw those pictures I barely recognized Sasha. If the caption hadn't had her name I wouldn't have believed it. She has feelings for this man. It was all over her," Nicole said.

"I think we all saw the same thing," Lynn said looking pointedly at B.J. "We can't let her just throw all that away. No matter what our feelings are on the situation."

"So I guess the question is who's gonna talk to her?" Safari asked.

All eyes fell on Cat. She bowed her head in resignation. After this one she would not meddle. She would leave it to little old women in Florida with blue hair.

"I will."

Her head snapped up.

Sindee Lynn

"I will talk to my sister. I saw the same thing you guys and half of Chicago saw. And despite how I feel about the situation, I would be less than a sister or a friend if I didn't try to get her to see reason."

Chapter 20

Sasha pushed her way through her front door, her arms heavy laden with more work from the office. She barely got the door closed before the files slipped out of her fingers onto the floor.

"Dammit," she yelled to the empty house.

She threw her briefcase to the floor and bent down to pick up the papers. It was Saturday and she had gone into the office for a few hours. Sasha grunted. Well it had started out as a few hours. It was after six now and she'd brought home several hours of work with her. She had to keep busy. If she didn't then thoughts she'd rather not think about would intrude and she'd go back to the crying mess she'd been for days after ending things with Dylan.

Having picked all the papers up, she carried them into her kitchen and tossed them on the island. She'd taken to working down here instead of in her office upstairs. Memories of Dylan were all throughout her home but they were stronger there. She'd made a space for him to share her large desk. They'd sit across from each other for hours working in silence until they're fingers would brush or they'd look up and find the other watching them. Then work would be the last thing on their minds.

Sasha felt the burn of familiar tears at the back of her throat. She strengthened her resolve. She would not cry over this. She would not. It had been two weeks and she was going to get over him. The first fat drop hit her hand and all she could do was stare as it was quickly followed by another.

"Oh shit," she cursed getting up to look for some tissues. She'd taken to hiding them all over the house because she never knew when the water works would start.

She'd found her stash in the pantry closet when her doorbell rang. She quickly blew her nose and wiped her eyes dry. God she hoped it was not Louis. Ever since the picture had run he'd become more and more amorous. Sasha had been ducking him for days.

"God if you're listening please don't let it be Louis."

Sasha opened her door. A deep sigh left her body. God was having a good laugh at her expense today.

"Are you gonna invite me in?" B.J. asked.

"If I said no would you go away," she asked blocking entry into her home. She'd been avoiding calls from her sister all week. She didn't feel up to hearing any reminders of what a mess she'd gotten herself into. She could do that all on her own.

"No," B.J. said standing her ground.

Another sigh left Sasha as she stepped back to allow her sister into her home. She walked back into the kitchen where she found her sister had already taken a seat at the island. B.J. was looking at the pile of folders she's brought home from the office.

"A little light reading."

"What do you want B.J.?"

She saw the deep breath her sister took and knew she was in for it. This was what she'd been avoiding. She'd rather it had been Louis at the door.

"I want you to start acting like the older sister and not the immature child you have been for the last two weeks."

"Huh?" was all Sasha could utter.

Okay not exactly the start she had predicted but she could only assume more was coming. And it was guaranteed she wouldn't like it.

"If this Dylan person is someone you want to be with then it's time you got off your ass and did something about it. Good men like that don't come around often and there's no guarantee he's going to wait for you forever."

"Huh?"

This was not the conversation she expected to get from her sister. Not only had she expected a lecture about propriety and how she could have been caught in such a compromising position she'd also expected to hear something about Dylan's being white. Sasha paused. Funny how she hadn't thought of that in a long time. Somewhere along the way the fact that Dylan was white stopped being an issue for her. He'd just become the man she was dating.

"I swear Sasha. I hope you had more conversation for Dylan than this. You sound like a broken record," B.J. snapped.

"We didn't do a lot of talking," she said under her breath.

At B.J.'s widened gaze, a small smile tugged at the corners of her mouth. It was the first real smile she'd given in a long time. She could never stop smiling while she was seeing Dylan. Just the thought of him could bring on the goofiest look.

"I gathered as much by the picture," B.J. retorted.

Her mouth opened in shock. Her sister had made a joke. Not something she was known for.

"Good one," Sasha said.

B.J. bowed her head.

"I've been hanging around Cat too long. Seems she's rubbing off on me in more ways than one."

That was very cryptic Sasha thought eyeing her sister. She was about to ask her when B.J. continued.

"Now back to you. Do you or do you not want this man?"

She opened her mouth to reply then closed it. Was this a trick question? Maybe there was a deeper meaning that she was missing. Regardless the answer was the same. Even after the worse possible thing happening it was still the same.

"Well yes but ..."

"Do you believe this man wants you in return?" B.J. continued, interrupting her when she would have said more.

That was definitely a no brainer. She thought back on the many messages Dylan had left her over the last two weeks. All asking her to take some time to think about what they had before she made her final decision. Messages that all ended in his telling her how much he missed her. Sasha hadn't been able to delete any of them.

"Yes, but there's no way this would ever ...."

"He's not Melvin, Sasha," B.J. said interrupting her.

A shiver ran down her spine at the mention of her ex-fiancé.

"Melvin couldn't handle the pressure of being with a woman like the one you were becoming. Confident and capable of trusting your own judgment. So he had to tear you down to make himself look and feel good. He tried to undermine your work and your accomplishments. And he said hurtful things about you. He didn't deserve you. And you didn't deserve what he put you through. And if there was any indication Dylan Matthews was another Melvin I'd be right there beside you ready to kick his ass. But he's not. Dylan didn't do this to you Sasha. He didn't take the picture that night in the parking garage. And he wasn't the one who made the decision to run it on the front page."

Sasha barely felt the pressure of B.J.'s hand on her arm. She was so deep in her own misery.

"Don't make him pay for the actions of someone else. Don't you think it's time you stopped letting Melvin have control over your life?"

B.J. got up and left, leaving Sasha sitting in the kitchen stewing in her own misery. She didn't know how long she sat like that before she got up and blindly walked over to the sofa and plopped down.

Could B.J. be right? Was that what she was doing? Letting Melvin run her life. All this time she'd thought she was the one in control. Always thinking on her actions before she made them and always within her rules. Rules that had been created after her breakup with Melvin. Old pain filled her chest as she allowed thoughts she'd believed long since buried to come back to the front.

Changing the Rules

Thinking back on it now, Sasha couldn't believe she'd thought of spending the rest of her life with Melvin. He'd seemed like the perfect man for her. It was funny how that perfect man had tried to ruin her.

She and Melvin had begun dating shortly after she'd first started working at Freeman Investments, her previous employer. For her it had been love at first sight. He had been a senior financial analyst with five years of experience under his belt and the kind of man every girl wanted to take home to Mom and Dad. With a dark chocolate complexion, Melvin stood at six feet three inches with muscles to go along with the height. He had often times surprised people with his knowledge of the financial industry.

In the beginning, things were great. Sasha had acquired the book knowledge from school but Melvin had helped her put all that learning into more practical use. Explaining the customer wasn't interested in fancy terms, they wanted to know the bottom line and that was how much money you were going to make them.

She had been a quick study. She'd always known she had a natural way with numbers but she'd learned she had a way with people as well. Her smile could put them at ease when handing over their life savings to her. She'd learned how to dress and style her hair to appear older, thus putting some of her older clients at ease with entrusting her with their money. It wasn't long before Melvin began recommending her to assist on some of the larger accounts he handled. That's when she had really begun to be noticed.

Two years had passed and their personal relationship grew stronger. Sasha had thought Melvin was the one. He understood what she did and knew the pressures of the job better than anyone. He could relate to having to stay at the office late. He was there right along side her most nights. But along with their personal relationship, Sasha's career grew as well. She had gained confidence in her own abilities and started overseeing her own projects. At first she had thought Melvin was happy for her. After all how could he not be? He had been her mentor in a way. But nonetheless, things began to get tense between them. And despite feeling the change in their relationship, Sasha hadn't wanted to believe the cause of it at the time. However, when she had gotten the lead for an account he had assumed he would get, she could no longer ignore the obvious.

Rumors began to circulate she had not gotten the assignment on her own merit. Since she was one of only three females in her department and the only black one, it was suggested she'd been handed the assignment simply because she was a black female. Sasha hadn't wanted to believe Melvin had been the source of those hurtful things.

Changing the Rules

After all he'd claimed to love her, but when she'd overheard him for herself. There was no way she could keep the blinders on any longer.

She had ended their relationship and Melvin had eventually left the company. A short time later she had been slapped in the face again with her own stupidity when she had been told he had tried to discredit the work she'd done on the last account they had worked on together. He'd claimed he'd done the brunt of the work himself when in fact the opposite had been true.

That was when her first rule had been created. Sasha figured she had made enough mistakes in her relationship with Melvin that as long as she didn't do any of them again she should be okay.

She absently wiped at the tears that had fallen. B.J. was right. She'd let her dealings with Melvin dictate every relationship after that. She had unknowingly given him more control over her after they'd broken up than when they'd been together. And she had never had a problem with that until Dylan. He'd contradicted every one of her rules right from the start. No matter how she tried to stay within her comfort zone, he just kept enticing her to step outside of it. And only when she let go had she discovered so much about herself. A giggle escaped Sasha. Who knew she was a closet freak? There was passion inside of her she'd never have known was there if not for Dylan, or perhaps it was only because of him that it was there. She'd had sex before but never had it been the uncontrollable thing it was with him. Melvin had even referred to her as an old maid on occasion after she'd failed to try something a little more adventurous. Another giggle escaped. If he only knew all the places she and Dylan had sex he would just die.

Sasha got up from her couch. She sat at the island, with pad and pen she wrote out her rules. Ripping the piece of paper out of her pad she headed upstairs to her office. Memories assailed her immediately and for the first time in two weeks she didn't fight them off. She wanted them to come.

She turned on her shredder. The quiet humming calmed her. Taking a deep breath she dropped the piece of paper which contained all her rules and watched it disintegrate into a thousand little pieces.

"Good bye Melvin," she said before hurrying to her bedroom for the phone. She didn't have much time.

Chapter 21

The nerves running through Sasha as she stepped from the limo's cool interior couldn't be described. She was terrified. What if things didn't go the way she wanted? What if he showed up with someone else? That thought almost had her getting back into the limo. But she took a deep calming breath and gave a weak smile to the man assisting her out of the vehicle. Her hand moved nervously to her hair and down the sides of her dress. You can do this, she told herself as she looked up at the steps in front of her.

"May I?"

The question was accompanied by an elegantly attired elbow pushed in her direction. Sasha smiled at the gentleman and nodded her consent. With each step she took closer to the door the butterflies in her stomach turned into birds in full flight. What if her name hadn't made it on the guest list after all? Oh god what if Dylan had asked that she be taken off? She glanced up to see they were at the door.

She thanked the gentleman beside her and took another deep breath. There was no turning back now.

"Good evening Madame. Your name?"

"Sasha Jordan," she managed to croak pass the lump in her throat.

It seemed like hours she waited as he flipped through the many lists. With each page flipped dread formed in the pit of her stomach the size of a boulder.

"Ah there you are Ms. Jordan," he said finally lifting his head to smile at her.

Sasha tried not to allow the relief she felt in the answering smile she gave him.

"Enjoy your evening," he said bowing slightly as he motioned her inside.

One hurdle crossed and another to go, she thought as she looked around in awe. There were no words to describe the elegance that surrounded her. Her gaze kept darting from one thing to the next not able to quite believe she was inside the mayor's mansion. Perhaps on another occasion she would have been able to fully enjoy the architecture surrounding her or the art on the walls, but she needed to find Dylan.

***

Sasha gently massaged her aching toes. She'd been searching for Dylan for what felt like hours and as of yet

Changing the Rules

had not managed to even catch sight of him. She had been headed to some of the smaller rooms when her feet had begged for mercy. She'd sat down at the first empty table. Hopefully she could gain feeling in her toes before she was forced to get up. Maybe she should have just called him instead of trying to be impulsive. It would have certainly been easier on her poor feet.

"Well has anyone found out who she is yet? I mean is she just some commoner hoping to catch the limelight or what?"

Her ears perked up at the sound of the female voice coming from behind her.

"I don't know but did you see the way she was clinging to him. It was almost indecent." Another female voice commented.

"I couldn't agree more but does anyone know who she is?" asked the first voice again.

A chair scrapped and a heavy sigh come from behind her.

"My feet are killing me. Who are we gossiping about ladies," asked the newcomer.

"Dylan Matthews of course who else. Have you seen him this evening? He hasn't left the bar all night," the second voice said a hint of sadness in her voice.

Sasha gasped.

"No but I saw the pictures. If only my Harry would look at me like that," the newcomer replied a sigh in her voice.

"Oh pooh. Who cares about that? It made her look like the tramp she most certainly is for being caught in a situation like that. You would never find my Tiffany in that position," the second voice said with disdain.

"Does anyone know where she came from? I've never seen her with him out anywhere before but then Dylan has been keeping to himself lately," asked the first lady.

"I think the paper says she works for Presco." The newcomer said.

"So that's it. Well, I should have known. It's just an office fling. Means nothing. I'm sure he'll be back to himself in no time. So I'll just let Tiffany know," the second voice said with a laugh.

"Gladys really give the poor boy some recovery time before you set Tiffany on him," the newcomer said with reproach. "Besides he may actually have had feelings for this one. It was all over them both in the pictures."

"Oh pooh," the lady Sasha now new to be Gladys replied. She could almost see her waving off the comments.

Changing the Rules

"It does all make sense now though. I imagine it would make it easier to have an afternoon tryst. Your office or mine," the first lady said laughing.

Sasha had heard enough. She shoved her sore feet back into her shoes and got up from the table embarrassment heating her face. This is what she'd been afraid of. People thought he'd hired her just so he could sleep with her. The nerve of those old bittys. Sasha headed towards the door. She was done. Then she stopped abruptly. Wait. She was doing it again. The same thing she had been doing for the last two weeks. Running. And she was tired of it. Those people didn't know her and in the long run they didn't matter. Dylan had been trying to get her to understand that as long as they knew what the truth was and her work spoke for itself then who cared what everyone else thought. She turned and headed towards the bar where Dylan was reported to be developing a relationship with the bartender. She only hoped that was the only relationship he'd developed since she'd seen him last.

Rounding the corner after asking directions to the bar, she breathed a sigh of relief. He was indeed at the bar. Dylan was leaning against the bar swirling a glass in one hand while another sat in front of him. He appeared to be speaking with the man beside him. Sasha walked a little closer, butterflies the size of eagles swirled in her stomach.

She took a deep breath and prayed she wouldn't be sick. She approached them from behind where they stood. When she heard their conversation she paused behind a large plant.

"So who did you bring tonight?" the man asked.

"No one," Dylan replied simply before downing the liquid from his glass. He put it down and reached for the other one sitting in front of him.

"I would have thought it would be the cute little number from the newspaper a few weeks ago?" the man asked.

"Nope," Dylan said taking a gulp of his fresh drink.

"Hmm and to think I actually thought she might be someone special," the guy commented.

Dylan finished off his drink before turning back to the man.

"Yeah what makes you say that Sean old buddy?"

Sasha heard the slur of Dylan's words. She wondered how much he'd had to drink.

"It was in the way you were looking at her in one of the pictures. And I guess the way you were touching her."

"Can I get another please," Dylan asked of the bartender. "Yeah well things change."

"I kind of figured. So you wanna tell me what happened?"

Changing the Rules

The expression on Dylan's face changed. His shoulders slumped as he leaned against the bar. When he lifted his eyes to look at his friend, her heart began to ache for all that she'd put him through. She could see the sadness reflected within their blue depths. There were dark shadows beneath them that spoke of sleepless nights.

"Things just didn't work out. I guess she decided I wasn't what she wanted after all."

Sean laughed.

"And since when did you let something like that stop you. You've never quit on something you wanted."

Dylan grunted.

"Yeah well I'm fighting a loosing battle. What can you do when everything about you goes against the *Rules of Love*," he said sarcasm dripping from his words.

Sasha straightened. How did he know about that? She tried to rack her brain to recall if she'd told him but came up blank.

"Have you tried begging?" Sean asked a serious expression on his face.

"Give me some credit," Dylan said finishing of another drink. "Of course I did. But it didn't help."

The man put his hand on Dylan's shoulder and squeezed.

"Just give her some time. She'll come around and see what a great guy you are."

The sadness in the look Dylan gave his friend put Sasha into action.

"I already know what a great guy he is," she said making her presence known. "I only hope he can forgive me for taking so long to figure it out."

Dylan's head snapped up. She felt his gaze rake over her body perhaps in an effort to assure himself he wasn't hallucinating.

"Sasha," he whispered.

"Well I can see I am no longer needed here," Sean said giving her small bow before walking away.

"What are you doing here" Dylan questioned.

She noticed he hadn't moved closer to her. He was still leaning against the bar. So she moved closer to him. When only a breath of space separated them she glanced up at him. The look of wariness tore at her heart.

"I wanted to say I'm sorry. Sorry for making you pay for the mistakes of someone else."

Tears clogged her throat, threatening to spill forth. Dammit as much as she'd cried in the last two weeks one would think she didn't have any left.

"I love you, Sasha," Dylan whispered close to her ear as he drew her to his chest. "I would never do anything to intentionally hurt you."

Sasha looked up at him and saw the love shining brightly in his eyes. The first tears began to fall from her eyes.

"I know that. I knew it then but I was just looking for any reason to run away from what I was feeling I guess. So when the pictures came out I used them as the perfect excuse. I'm so sorry Dylan."

She pulled him tighter against her and whispered the words her heart had been singing for weeks, maybe even since the first day she'd seen him.

"I love you Dylan Matthews."

Dylan pulled back and stared into her eyes. For once Sasha didn't try to hide her feelings. She allowed them to show from the depths of her soul.

"I think we should leave because if you keep looking at me like that I will be forced to take you to one of this mansion's many bedrooms and have makeup sex that will really give them something to talk about."

A shiver ran through her body at the thought. It had been a long two weeks and her body had missed his.

"Um before we go," she said turning to give him a mischievous look flashing in her brown eyes. "Do you know a Gladys who has a daughter named Tiffany?"

Dylan frowned in confusion but nodded his head.

Sasha grabbed his hand and headed them away from the bar back in the direction she'd come from.

"Good. I'd like to meet Gladys. I'll explain on the way. Then we can leave and have all the make up sex we both can handle."

Chapter 22

Dylan watched Sasha cross the parking lot and enter the building. He rushed over to the building's maintenance supervisor to make sure everything was ready.

"Are we all set Harold?" he asked with a pat on the man's back.

"That we are Mr. Matthews. Good luck to ya," Harold said and walked away shaking his head and chuckling. Wait 'til he got home and told Margie, his wife of more than thirty years, about this. Being the softy she is she'd think it the most romantic thing.

Dylan moved to stand behind one of the big artificial trees in the lobby. He had been planning this for weeks. His timing had to be perfect. Just then he saw Sasha enter the building and head towards the elevator. God, but she looked gorgeous today. She wore a black skirt that stopped just below her knees. He could see the hint of a blue blouse peeking out from the collar of her black cropped jacket. He loved the color blue on her. His hungry gaze traveled down her slender body and stopped when he noticed a large amount of leg showing as she walked. His blood started to boil as he got another peak of leg. The closer she got he noticed the reason. There was a split in her long skirt that had to run from mid thigh down the length of the skirt. What was she trying to do kill him? No, better yet he decided as he noticed he was not the only one watching her cross the lobby, she was trying to get someone else killed.

    Dylan saw Sasha halt before the elevator doors and appeared to be reading the sign. *"Lobby elevators closed for maintenance. Please use the alternate elevators located at the other end of the building."*

***

    Sasha couldn't believe this. How could they shut down the elevators in a building that had over fifty floors? Sure she could walk all the way to the other side as they suggested, but geez. She looked down at the shoes she had worn today. Not a good way to go anyway you looked at it and the stairs, which were right beside the elevators, were a definite no. How tacky would it be for her to take her shoes off and walk to the other side of the building to catch the elevator? She was weighing the pros and cons when she saw a man walk up in a maintenance uniform and remove the sign.

Changing the Rules

"Excuse me does this mean the elevators are okay and back on?" she asked praying he would say yes.

"Yes ma'am. We are all done with the maintenance," the man replied and pressed the up button for her. When the doors swooshed open he gave a slight bow and waved her in. "Your chariot awaits ma'am," he said with a huge smile.

Sasha smiled back at him and entered the elevator. "Thank you kind sir."

She pressed the button for her floor. The doors were closing, when a foot thrust itself between the closing doors.

"I would have waited," Sasha mumbled under her breath, not believing anyone could be that stupid. Didn't they know the elevators didn't care about body parts?

When the doors opened to reveal Dylan standing there smiling at her, Sasha swatted him with her hand.

"You idiot. Don't you know that's dangerous?" she asked now smiling too.

Just the sight of him had her heart pounding in her chest as if she'd run a race of some kind. Even after all these months it never ceased to amaze her. One would think after almost eight months of dating and seeing each other on a daily basis it would eventually get old. But as of yet it was still just like she were seeing him for the first time.

"No amount of pain is too great to endure if it means I can be alone with you. And good morning to you as well gorgeous," he said, pulling her into his arms and kissing her soundly on the lips.

She reached around his neck to pull him closer. As their kiss deepened she played with his hair, which now touched his shoulders. He'd let it grow out since she'd told him he looked sexier that way.

"Wow," she said still wrapped in his arms. "What a way to start the day. Good morning to you as well."

"A better way would have been for us to wake up this morning in each other's arms," Dylan said running his fingers through her hair.

"I couldn't agree more, but you didn't get back into town until early this morning. It was too late for me to drive over there and I wouldn't hear of your taking the long drive to me. You were exhausted when you called to tell me you were back in town."

"You could have just been there waiting for me when I got home. I gave you a key months ago. One I feel it necessary to remind you that you refuse to use. I gave it to you for times like last night Sash. I still don't understand why you refuse to use it," he said kissing her on the temple. His roaming hands moving from her hair down the slim line of her back to cup her firm butt cheeks in his hands.

Changing the Rules

Sasha sighed, closing her eyes. She dropped her head on his chest and kissed his chin. This was an old argument with them. She had told him repeatedly ... bump ... thump ... her eyes flew open. What the hell?

The elevator had stopped its upward rise. Okay, Sasha said to herself, I will not panic.

"Uh Dylan tell me the elevator didn't just stop," she said raising worried brown eyes to gaze into Dylan's much brighter blue ones.

"Yes, I do believe it has," he said nonchalantly. His hands gripped her ass a little firmer and pulled her closer to his hardening body.

"Stop that," she told him trying to pull out of his embrace. What was wrong with him? The elevator had stopped.

"Shouldn't we call somebody or something? Don't they have one of those phones in here?" she asked trying to remain calm, but all she could think about was the elevator drop in that movie about the speeding bus with the bomb under it.

Dylan loosened his grip on her slightly and glanced over his shoulder.

"Yeah I guess there is one."

Sasha looked up at him as if he had lost his mind. Why wasn't he calling somebody to get them out of here?

Well, if he wouldn't then she would. She pulled out of Dylan's arms and moved towards the emergency phone, but he merely pulled her back into his embrace and secured his hold around her slim waist.

"What's your rush? Besides you didn't answer my question."

Sasha frowned up at him. "What question?"

Dylan gave a sigh of impatience.

"You were about to tell me why you refuse to use your key to my house," he said placing a kiss on her wrinkled nose.

Here they were stuck on god only knows what floor in an elevator and he was talking about house keys. It was confirmed he had lost his mind.

"Dylan in case you hadn't noticed we really have a bigger issue to worry about right now."

Dylan shook his head at her and bent down to touch his forehead to hers.

"Right now the only thing I am concerned about is your issue with my house keys. So come on tell me."

Sasha gave a sigh of frustration. Maybe if she told him for the hundredth time he would stop this nonsense and they could get out of here.

"I don't believe we're having this conversation again and at a time like this."

Changing the Rules

"Sasha just answer the question."

"The reason I don't use your house key is because the house is just that. It's yours. I don't feel I have a right to just come and go as I please. I would feel like I was intruding in your personal space," she said.

Dylan simply grinned at her monotone answer.

"And if you had every right to intrude on my personal space?"

"What?" she asked the frown between her brows deepening.

"I said, and if you had every right to intrude on my personal space. What then?"

"Dylan there is no way I would ever feel like that unless I lived there. And before you ask, I am not shacking up with you. My mother and father adore you but they would both have heart attacks if I moved in with you. That is after my father had killed you for compromising his daughter. And I for one would like to have them and you around for a little bit longer."

The smile he gave her confirmed what she'd been thinking. He had lost his mind. They needed to find a way out of this elevator.

"I am not suggesting we shack up," he said finally releasing her from his arms.

Maybe the close quarters was cutting off oxygen to his brain because he wasn't making any sense at all. Just then she looked at Dylan and noticed he was lowering himself to the elevator floor. Her mouth opened in a perfect 'o' and not one word came out. Her brain had stopped processing any more thoughts other than to question why he was on his knee in front of her with a black box.

Dylan took Sasha's cold fingers in his and rubbed his thumb along the back of it, causing more butterflies to take flight in her already quivering insides. Tears pooled in the corners of her eyes as she continued to glance down at the beautiful man kneeling before her. Her heart was so full of love for him.

"Sasha, I have loved you from the moment I saw you on this very elevator all those months ago. And in the last several months that love has only grown. You have come into my life and given it meaning again. Everyday I see you and I know in my heart with you is where I belong. Sasha Bernadette Jordan will you marry me?"

Sasha felt the tears falling from her eyes and didn't try to stop them. She touched the side of his face. When his gaze met hers, she saw tears shining in the brilliant blue eyes gazing back at her.

"Yes. All day every day yes."

Changing the Rules

With shaking hands he lifted the velvet box to reveal the most beautiful ring she had ever seen. An emerald cut diamond winked up at her. Never in her wildest dreams had she ever imagined a ring like the one Dylan was placing on her finger. He rose to his feet and lifted her in his arms. He twirled her around the small confines of the elevator, stumbling when the elevator began moving again. He pinned her against the elevator wall.

"You know that first morning I saw you on this elevator this is what I wanted to do," he said against her parted lips.

Sasha reached around him and hit the stop button. She slowly unbuttoned her jacket, letting it fall to the floor. When she reached for the buttons on her blouse she lifted her gaze to Dylan's, whose eyes were glued to her hands.

"We wasted the first ride. Let's not waste this one."

The End